Ireland Into Film

Series editors:
Keith Hopper (text) and Gráinne Humphreys (images)

Ireland Into Film is the first project in a number of planned collaborations between Cork University Press and the Irish Film Institute. The general aim of this publishing initiative is to increase the critical understanding of 'Irish' Film (i.e. films made in, or about, Ireland). This particular series brings together writers and scholars from the fields of Film and Literary Studies to examine notable adaptations of Irish literary texts.

Other titles available in this series:

The Dead (Kevin Barry)
December Bride (Lance Pettitt)
This Other Eden (Fidelma Farley)

(Colin MacCabe)

Ireland Into Film

FELICIA'S JOURNEY

Stephanie McBride

CORK UNIVERSITY PRESS

in association with
THE IRISH FILM INSTITUTE

First published in 2006 by
Cork University Press
Cork
Ireland

British Library Cataloguing in Publication Data
A CIP catalogue record for this book is available from the British Library.

ISBN-10: 1-85918-399-9
ISBN-13: 978-185918-399-1

Typesetting by Red Barn Publishing, Skeagh, Skibbereen
Printed by ColourBooks Ltd, Baldoyle, Dublin

Ireland Into Film receives financial assistance from
the Arts Council/An Chomhairle Ealaíon and the Irish Film Institute

Irish Film Institute

Items should be returned on or before the last date shown below. Items not already requested by other borrowers may be renewed in person, in writing or by telephone. To renew, please quote the number on the barcode label. To renew online a PIN is required. This can be requested at your local library. Renew online @ **www.dublincitypubliclibraries.ie** Fines charged for overdue items will include postage incurred in recovery. Damage to or loss of items will be charged to the borrower.

Leabharlanna Poiblí Chathair Bhaile Átha Cliath
Dublin City Public Libraries

Dublin City
Baile Átha Cliath

Brainse Bhaile Thormod
Ballyfermot Library

Tel. 6269324/5

Date Due	Date Due	Date Due
20 OCT 07		

CONTENTS

LIST OF ILLUSTRATIONS

Acknowledgements

Keith Hopper, for his clear and encouraging editorial assistance; Gráinne Humphreys of the Irish Film Institute for her enthusiastic good humour in her suggestions and trawl for images; research students Justin Carville, Maeve Connolly and Orla Ryan for the stimulating discussions; a special thanks to Martin Gale for generous permission to reproduce his painting in black and white; I would also like to acknowledge the diverse and unique input of James Armstrong, Bernadette Comerford, Michael Foley, Luke Gibbons, Karl Grimes, Tanya Kiang, Dolores MacKenna, Jean O'Halloran, Niamh O'Sullivan, Kevin Rockett, and finally Mick Cunningham for endless love and joy.

The editors would also like to thank Emma Barker, Icon Film Distribution, Mary Fox (Penguin Group), Ruth Carroll, Royal Hibernian Academy, William Gallagher, Ben Cloney, Deirdre Dolan, Kazandra O'Connell and the staff of the Irish Film Archive, Siobhán Farrell, Eclipse Pictures, Seán Ryder and Sara Wilbourne.

INTRODUCTION:
SOCIAL AND CULTURAL CONTEXTS

At that time she used to go for walks with a boy who whispered often that he loved her, until one night, behind the Electricity Works he had taken liberties with her unresisting body and afterwards had whispered nothing more at all. (William Trevor, *Mrs Eckdorf in O'Neill's Hotel*, 1969)[1]

Felicia's Journey, William Trevor's thirteenth novel, was first published in 1994. It tells the story of a young Irishwoman who travels to England in search of the father of her unborn child, unaware that he is a soldier in the British army. Disorientated in her new surroundings, she encounters Mr Hilditch, who befriends her and helps her in her search. Outwardly affable, *Felicia's Journey* reveals a darker side to this genial monster. Under the guise of assisting her in the search for her lover, Johnny Lysaght, Hilditch proceeds to deceive her, stealing her meagre funds and forcing her total dependence on him. His predatory grasp extends to control of her body, as he eventually persuades her to abort her child. While she gains increasing knowledge and finally realises that Hilditch has made a life out of befriending and murdering lost young girls, she evades their fates to make another life for herself – having travelled far from her family and small-town community. Moving through the anonymity of the city, *Felicia's Journey* closes on an image of serenity and calm.

In the short period between the time the novel was written and the time Canadian director Atom Egoyan began filming his adaptation, Ireland clearly underwent major historical, political, social and economic changes. By the time of the cinema release in 1999,

Ireland's 'Celtic Tiger'[2] economic boom was in full swing. This in turn marked – and in many respects also prompted – a series of rapid shifts that would irrevocably alter the country's social and cultural landscape, as reflected in such phenomena as:

- accelerated economic development, accompanied by a rise in consumption and the globalising impact of large brand chains at the micro level. In a highly visible way, this began to change the streetscapes not only of cities but also of provincial towns – they were now dotted with Centra/Spar/Super-Valu stores which were already beginning to encroach on Felicia's world, displacing the small, local and family businesses;
- the beginning of a hyper-saturation of tourism;
- major growth of mobile-phone usage; and
- increased mobility, through the growth in the 'no-frills' travel culture, bringing overseas destinations much closer.

In addition, the period saw a significant decline in the influence of the Roman Catholic Church, which experienced a string of scandals. One case in 1993, in which the Bishop of Galway admitted to having had an affair and fathering a son, was later followed by a series of revelations of clerical abuse which continue to reverberate into the twenty-first century. The 'X case' of 1993, which sought to prevent a teenager from travelling abroad to procure an abortion, adds a further social and historical dimension to Felicia's fictional journey. These events followed a decade in which the Republic of Ireland's citizens had voted to introduce a constitutional ban on abortion; an unmarried mother lost her teaching job because she was pregnant; a teenager died alone while giving birth in a grotto in rural Ireland; and there was an alleged case of infanticide in rural Kerry which came to be known as the 'Kerry Babies' case.

Significantly, too, there were major population changes,[3] with the country experiencing a huge upsurge in inward migration for the first time in the modern era (see Table 1).

Table 1: Population of the Republic of Ireland[4]

Year	Population
1901	3,221,823
1951	2,960,593
1961	2,818,341
1971	2,978,248
1981	3,443,405
1991	3,525,719
1996	3,626,087
2002	3,917,203

An image towards the end of Fergus Tighe's 1987 film, *Clash of the Ash*, in which the main character leaves his home town in County Cork for work abroad, resonates in the image in the film of *Felicia's Journey* when her boyfriend, Johnny Lysaght, catches the bus out of town to return to his British army barracks. In 1990s Ireland, however, migration was no longer largely a one-way flow of traffic to the 'colonies'. By the end of the decade this had evolved into a more dynamic two-way flow. While Felicia's journey in 1994 leads to her exile in England (echoing previous generations of Irish experiences), a substantial reverse trend of inward migration to Ireland in the last decade of the twentieth century was changing her version of Ireland for ever.

Perhaps the question may then be posed: is *Felicia's Journey* (the film) already, in a significant sense, a period piece? 'Period' in the same sense as, for example, Mike Leigh's *Vera Drake* (2004), a film offering insights into the social tremors of a past era, rather than presenting a spectacle of exquisite period detail associated with the 'heritage cinema' genre or, in Alan Parker's memorable phrase, 'the Laura Ashley school of film making'.[5]

At the same time as the Republic was beginning to experience this economic upturn, the island's political landscape was undergoing a

3

radical shift. On 31 August 1994, the IRA announced 'a complete cessation of military activities'. The following month, London lifted its broadcasting ban against Sinn Féin and in October 1994 the Combined Loyalist Military Command announced its ceasefire. In April 1998 Northern Ireland's parties signed up for the historic Good Friday Agreement and the following month a referendum saw 71 per cent supporting the deal in Northern Ireland. So, while Trevor's novel portrays a rigid Republicanism whose honour is dealt a double-blow because the (grand)child Felicia is carrying is fathered by Johnny Lysaght, who has joined the British army – still the occupying force, in her father's eyes – the impact of the changing political field meant that the history of Irishmen serving in the British army in different eras was retrieved and acknowledged. So much so, in fact, that full funeral honours were accorded to an Irish soldier from Dublin who was killed while serving in the British army in the Gulf War in 2003.[6]

In this context, then, this very shift in the social and cultural landscape during the decade raises certain issues for the production of the novel's adaptation for the big screen. But while the novel is clearly an Irish one, a story about Ireland and Irish matters, in most senses the film adaptation is not an Irish film. The most global of industries, film has always been international in its production, distribution and reception and *Felicia's Journey* is no exception. It demonstrates this international production economy very clearly: a novel written by William Trevor (the most English of Irishmen), adapted and directed by Atom Egoyan (a Canadian Armenian), and funded by Icon Productions, a company founded by Mel Gibson which is 'funded by the studios but independent of them'.[7]

With an established international profile as a director within the independent sector, Egoyan's work is characterised by a recurrent interest in certain themes – identity, memory, desire, voyeurism and exhibitionism – as well as a commitment to visual possibilities offered by the media age. Like Trevor, who has also referred to himself as an 'outsider',[8] Egoyan's work is permeated by a sense of foreignness and alienation. With critical acclaim for his own projects, Egoyan had already tackled adaptation with Russell Banks' *The Sweet Hereafter*, which won the Grand Jury Prize at the 1997 Cannes Film Festival.

Speaking about film adaptation, Egoyan catches the tensions involved in this process: 'It's that balance of trying to respect and honour the spirit of their work, but also feeling free to reinvent and to find a way of reinterpreting it, which makes the process of adaptation organic and urgent.'[9]

It is also a matter of the film-making apparatus, which involves not only scripting and adapting the novel but visualising it through casting, setting and location. For example, in casting Bob Hoskins as the serial killer Hilditch, Egoyan indicates his awareness of the international dimension of the industry:

Bob has a different reputation outside of the United Kingdom . . . he's an actor who is immediately accessible . . . it's brilliant for a role like this where the character is so duplicitous and has invented this entire mythology for himself.[10]

Hoskins also invests the film with intertextual nuances, which will be discussed later. Casting Elaine Cassidy – an unknown and fresh in global industrial terms – as Felicia is more to do with capturing the innocent demeanour of her character and an Ireland which is definitively pre-Celtic Tiger. Egoyan himself explains in several interviews about the film – including the director's commentary on the DVD release – that the Ireland of the novel no longer exists.

Egoyan also comments specifically on the politics and history of place when he refers to the difficulty of finding a suitable location for shooting the Irish scenes, because the impact of tourism had prompted a 'heritage' make-over in many small towns and villages. Eventually he settled on Glansworth in County Cork.[11] But a further significant issue emerges in finding a visual idiom which can generate the sense of place, not only geographically and historically for international audiences but also in terms of expressing emotional states. Compression is always a feature of the adaptation process, and theories of adaptation consistently note this – generally in terms of narrative/character compression. In Egoyan's film, different registers within the visual economy of his film translate as a kind of visual compression, a shorthand for international viewers, signalling a recognisable Irish setting – with familiar emblems of castles and ruins which underpin the narrative's concern with the stranglehold of Irish history – with its ancestral voices and scarred tissue of the land. That the compression also involves an evacuation or reduction of some of the novel's themes exercises some commentators.

Certainly, Trevor's novel clearly locates Hilditch within an imperial past, the story becoming an allegory for the troubled Anglo-Irish history which permeates the novel (and, indeed, much of Trevor's other fiction, including his short stories). The depth of the novel's writing raises questions about the extent to which this trope can be translated or articulated in a film for a global marketplace/audience, one which is less familiar with the intricacies of Ireland's colonial past and even its more recent history. Yet, arguably, as the title of this series, *Ireland into Film*, suggests, it is the process (rather than any direct or fixed symmetrical relationship) of articulation and transposition of Ireland – its social and cultural shifts – into the most global of art forms which can open up the ongoing dynamics of cultural identity and interpretation.

Egoyan was also acutely aware of the specific tone of Trevor's writing, which had a 'slightly absurdist and humorous' aspect.[12] Yet the tyranny of the moving image increases the difficulties of finding a tonal equivalence for finely nuanced writing. Trevor's fiction is frequently tinged with a wry humour. Occasionally, Hilditch's turn of phrase, such as his description of paying for Felicia's abortion as 'his treat', strikes the reader as oddly comic – as though it is the equivalent of a cup of tea and a scone. Trevor's 'woman dentist

[who] has dedicated her life to the rotten teeth of derelicts' (*FJ*, p. 213)[13] provides another humorous example, not easily translated in visual terms.

A darker aspect of the novel is the figure of the incestuous mother, whose transgression has shattered her son's life, and which presents another major problem of transposition for the screen narrative: 'The problem with adapting the book is that if you touch on incest, it becomes very heavy-handed.'[14] Egoyan further explains that he created the TV cook character (Gala) as the mother to imply something of their relationship. A later section of this essay will explore the subtexts of the relationship between food and consumption.

Moving Across Media

Marshall McLuhan developed a set of laws to analyse media culture.[15] Termed the 'tetrad', it involved four laws, presented as a series of questions:

1   What does the medium or technology extend?
2   What does it make obsolete?
3   What is retrieved?
4   What does the technology reverse it to if it is over-extended?

These are particular 'laws' to describe the evolution of media. Obviously an adaptation of a text from one medium into another medium – in particular, in our case, from novel to feature film – does not adhere to the same laws. Yet McLuhan's tetrad offers a touchstone in exploring how a text is 'translated' and transformed from one medium to another. We can ask a similar set of questions, such as:

1   What does the adaptation add or extend?
2   What does it make obsolete or subtract?
3   What is retrieved? What is amplified?
4   What does it reverse when it is over-extended?

While not intended as exhaustive, such questions can underpin the exploration of the film adaptation. Rather than looking for how 'faithful' the adaptation is in a limited and 'literal' sense of a one-to-one mapping, they invite a focus which opens out and stresses the evolutionary dynamic of the textual properties within the wider context of production, which carries within it the potential reception/audience for the text.

Trevor himself has alluded to the influence of film on the process of fiction-writing: 'You change the order of scenes. You remove what has become clutter . . . You can splice your fiction using scissors and glue.' He is also keenly aware of the issues involved in the trafficking between media: 'Raiding the world of film may be a productive exercise for the fiction writer, but when the raiding is the other way round it's not nearly as agreeable an experience.' He also recognises the shifts in emphasis involved in a shift in ownership of the literary property: 'It [the novel] may be squeezed where it shouldn't be squeezed, expanded where it shouldn't be expanded, smartened up with a bit of sleaze, made visually exciting when it should be shadowy, and have an upbeat ending tacked on.'[16]

Egoyan's initial plan to relocate the story of Felicia's journey to Canada (as a journey from Quebec to the west coast) indicates the porous quality of the text, although it would have substantially altered the tone and political dimensions of Trevor's novel – over-extending it, perhaps, despite some similarities between Canada's proximity to a dominant global culture and Ireland's own dominated status.

In their introduction to their edited collection of essays on *Subtitles*, Egoyan and Balfour write: 'Every film is a foreign film, foreign to some audience somewhere – and not simply in terms of language.'[17] Given the global nature of cinema, an accented film, in the words of Hamid Naficy, 'is made in the interstices and astride several cultures and languages'.[18] Egoyan was not only engaged in the adaptation of Trevor's original novel, reworking the textual cues, developing a visual idiom, but he was also – especially in the case of this novel – evolving a means of representing a sense of time and place, both Hilditch's and Felicia's. And although Egoyan suggests that the character of Felicia seems caught in the nineteenth century and Hilditch arrested in the 1950s,[19] arguably they are much closer in time, with a 1950s Ireland shaping Felicia's identity and ways of seeing.

The film production process, in a wider context, also exerts its own set of time/space compressions. If the landscape of the new Ireland presented challenges for a period piece, the English Midlands had also changed from the Dickensian images elaborated in the novel. As Egoyan himself puts it:

> I had this image of the Black Country, chimneys spewing out thick smoke, soot falling over people and dark satanic mills, and that's just not there any more . . . you're confronted with a quite anonymous setting.[20]

Yet the Birmingham of the film sustained recognisable features – firmly locating the film in a specific place.[21]

If, as David Lodge has suggested, a novel that is to be adapted is 'a basis for discussion, negotiation and revision',[22] then it's clear that Egoyan's film adaptation illustrates this – with its diverse skeins of his own authorial preoccupations, his idiomatic visual style and his creative additions – even within such an industrialised activity as film production.

Intertextuality

Writing in his extensive study of adaptation, *Novel to Film*, Brian McFarlane addresses the constantly vexed encumbrance of any adaptation:

> At every level from newspaper reviews to longer essays in critical anthologies and journals, the adducing of fidelity to the original novel as a major criterion for judging the film

adaptation is pervasive. No critical line is in greater need of re-examination – and devaluation.[23]

Complementing this position, intertextuality is another way of thinking about the process of adaptation. A central concept in contemporary literary and cultural studies, intertextuality dislodges the notion of a text having any independent or single meaning. Instead it emphasises a network of textual connections – in the words of Roland Barthes: 'Etymologically, the text is a tissue, a woven fabric.'[24] Avoiding the gridlock of an inert fidelity to its original, Egoyan's film offers insight into its source text, an interpretation which, as we shall see, also acts as an extended intertextual commentary on Trevor's novel.

2

NARRATIVE IMAGE: COVER VERSIONS

Perhaps you started leafing through the book already in the shop. Or were you unable to, because it was wrapped in its cocoon of cellophane? Now you are on the bus, standing in the crowd, hanging from a strap by your arm, and you begin undoing the package with your free hand, making movements something like a monkey, a monkey who wants to peel a banana and at the same time cling to the bough. (Italo Calvino, *If on a Winter's Night a Traveller*, 1979)[25]

A common adage is that you don't judge a book by its cover. Yet it is obvious that many book readers, buyers and sellers do just that. And it is clear that a book's cover design has to do a lot of work nowadays. It plays a significant role in the contemporary promotional economy. It provides an insight into the generic and narrative content through the design and selection of its text and image. It frequently carries extracts from reviews of the book and other works by the same author. And in many instances it is the first contact point, the initial interface between the reader and the text. In its address, in which it not only has to compete with other book covers on the particular shelf – or increasingly on the webpage – but with the vast array of other publications, the book cover image is a valuable measure of how the publisher attempts to position the novel. Its various reprints offer further indicators of the publisher's drive to reposition the novel – for example, to tie in with a later cinematic or television version. They chronicle a journey that the text itself makes as it goes through later adaptations and guises, reflecting the changing relationships between the novel and its readers – and the marketing department. Writing about book cover design, Alan Powers even goes as far as to assert

Plate 1. The cover of the first edition, 1994

that good covers carry a form of hidden eroticism, in order to say: 'Take me, I am yours.'[26]

The novel *Felicia's Journey* was first published in 1994 in hardback. In what John Ellis referred to as the 'narrative image'[27] in the context of film promotion, the mode of address on the cover on this first edition presents its themes sparingly (Plate 1). The entire surface of the cover features a grainy image of an industrial landscape. In the foreground is a field of unkempt grass, with a silhouette of a tree on the left edge, and in the middle distance are four cooling towers (not unlike the towers in the later film version) and three tall chimneys. Large clouds of white smoke billow skywards. In a text box is the title of the novel and in larger type size the author's name. In an overall grey cast, the only trace of human agency and personal scale is a discarded item of clothing which is visible in the bottom right corner. In terms of offering a sense of the novel's content, the image locates her journey within a nondescript, industrial landscape – the only hint of instability lies in this discarded clothing, which may yet be innocent and incidental. The emphasis here, which is made explicit in the pages of the novel itself, is the alienating experience of the industrial environment and of the boundaries between the field and the factory belt. There is sparse information as to the generic style, although it is possible to see the discarded scarf/handkerchief as a clue to flight or disappearance within the traditional conventions of mystery and crime fiction. The blurb on the back cover emphasises the author's power as a writer and the 'emotional energy required to read him'.

The absence of any human figures is continued on the covers of later editions of the novel, as well as an expansion of the visual trope of discarded garments. In a 1994 edition of the novel, the image which occupies two-thirds of the cover's surface is a nocturnal one. Caught in the yellow glare of headlights are garments strewn along the dark road. The image is charged with storytelling potential and deploys conventions associated with the thriller genre (*Blood Simple*, for example) to suggest a hasty dispatch, some form of disruption. This cover's textual information emphasises the author's name; a much smaller font announces in capital letters that this is 'A NOVEL',

Plate 2.   The cover of the 1999 film tie-in edition

but the cover lacks any signifiers at a textual level as to generic style, relying on the enlarged image of the nocturnal road scene to set the enigma as to who Felicia is and the nature of her journey. That the narrative involves the darker tones of human interaction, through tapping into conventions of crime fact and fiction (images of clothing, scene-of-crime details), is suggested while retaining an openness.

In an Australian edition from 1996, the same image is used, occupying three-quarters of the cover's surface. The top third of the cover now accords visual emphasis to the author's name through font size, while, underneath 'NATIONAL BESTSELLER' (in capital letters) and in small type above the author's name, a review extract indicates its thriller dimension as well as its psychological aspect. Anchoring the image is the novel's title – a handwriting font now replaces the classic serif type – and in smaller type 'A NOVEL' is again indicated in capital letters. The choice of stylised script invests the title and the narrative image with a human quality, suggesting a personal account, a diary of an itinerary perhaps.

All these cover images in their visual style offer a narrative image which distinguishes them from other novel styles by avoiding certain visual tropes associated with genres such as romantic fiction or the tendency in certain publishing houses to use fine art images in the design of book covers.[28] Yet a far more pertinent shift in the narrative image comes with later editions of the novel published as tie-ins with the film adaptation, and the covers issued on VHS/DVD. Versions of the novel published following the film's release (Plate 2) deploy images from the film but offer quite different readings and expectations of the book's narrative contents when viewed alongside the DVD/VHS covers.

This book cover's surface is almost entirely occupied by an image which shows a young woman's face (that of Elaine Cassidy, who played Felicia in Egoyan's film) superimposed on an image of the foam trail left in the wake of a ship's passage. The woman's face, eyes downcast, pensive and preoccupied, is an image from the film. In this cover construction, she appears to reflect while looking down at the stormy sea – the dividing line as she crosses from familiar home ground to alien culture – and at the same time the image overlaps her features upon the sea's waves. Almost imperceptible is another superimposition, at the top left of the cover, of a pair of eyes –

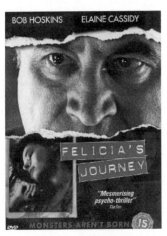

Plate 3.   DVD cover

Plate 4. VHS cover

embedded in the waves of a choppy sea – staring, focused. They are the eyes of Bob Hoskins, who played the character of Hilditch, the serial killer in the film. Even less noticeable at first glance is another eye, this time in the waves directly below the woman's face (and this time the person the eye belongs to is unclear). Both the author's name and the title are superimposed at the bottom of the cover, in strips of typeface replicating the Dymo labelling system used in the film. A final line in small sans-serif type, 'Now a film by Atom Egoyan', completes the textual information. This is a somewhat curious composition, given the generic frame and story. While film and television tie-ins frequently rely on star personas as a marketing strategy in cover design, these are generally anchored by further textual information – review extracts, tag lines. This composite of film images, despite its size, evades much of the film's narrative content and generic context. Curiously, too, the more familiar face of Bob Hoskins is eschewed, apart from the pair of eyes almost buried within the seascape. The image of vulnerability and innocence of Felicia's character as presented here floats free of any clear narrative context.

It could indicate a romance narrative, and there is little to indicate a thriller narrative – nor is it possible to locate it geographically.

In contrast to this is the design of one of the DVD cover images (Plate 3). A black background, with Artisan DVD at the top, followed by the Dymo strip lettering with the film's title, *Felicia's Journey*, followed below in smaller type by 'A film by Atom Egoyan'. Bob Hoskins in the character of Hilditch looks outwards, taking up the upper right corner of the image, while an image of Elaine Cassidy as Felicia in which she appears to be asleep occupies the lower left corner. The menacing aspect of Hoskins' staring eyes is accompanied by the following text alongside his face: 'The richest, most provocative serial killer movie in cinema history.' Apart from the superlatives, it clearly signals its sub-genre in cinema through the text and anchors the images of both characters/stars. Other DVD/VHS editions (Plate 4) include the text 'Monsters aren't born', and use the torn photograph with its ripped and jagged connotations to frame Hilditch/Hoskins' features, hinting at his voyeuristic and violent inclinations, while the image of Felicia/Cassidy is framed inside a clean, even border (though not quite clean and white, to be a Polaroid image), its lower position suggesting his predatory gaze down upon her as she sleeps oblivious of this.

The textual journey of the cover images has a clear trajectory at one level: it moves from a position where the literary address is prominent to one in which the author of the novel is entirely eclipsed – in one DVD cover image, there is now absolutely no reference to the novel's author. Amplified on some levels and omitted at another, it reflects and reinforces the novel's bumpy transition as a property within the media industries – the narrative image adapted for its positioning within different media registers and assumed audiences.

IN THE FIRST PLACE:
WILLIAM TREVOR'S FICTIONAL LANDSCAPE

What secrets are locked away behind that tapestry of fascinating windows?
What thoughts and voices occupy those rooms?
Here in my favourite part of Ireland reality is transformed by the escape from it. (William Trevor, *Hidden Ground*, 1990)[29]

Despite living outside Ireland since 1954, William Trevor's fictional worlds reveal a consistently vivid quality in his imaginings of the small towns of rural Ireland. He presents the stories of diverse characters whose lives are bound up with and often bounded by the everyday roles and functions of their local community. From Bridie's stoic acceptance that 'you can't change the way things are' in 'The Ballroom of Romance' to the McDowds' painful realisation of their exploitation by the English journalist, Hetty Fortune, in 'Events at Drimaghleen', the intensity of the fictional world comes through Trevor's careful prose in which he is alert to the power of keenly observed detail. This often takes the form of naming and listing familiar brands – perhaps an echo from his early days in the advertising industry – as well as an intense knowledge and familiarity with the shape and sensibility of small-town Ireland, its small shops and its local industries, the small badges of social class and the harbingers of change.

In *Felicia's Journey*, Trevor touches on many of his established themes and concerns. A sense of place, which is characteristic of his fiction, is a central force in the story and, significantly, it is a sense of place in emotional as well as historical and geographical terms. The novel tells how Felicia, a young Irish woman living in rural Ireland, goes in search of Johnny Lysaght, a soldier in the British army, the father of her unborn child, whom she believes is working in a lawnmower factory in the English Midlands. Adrift and disorientated in a foreign place, she is befriended by Mr Hilditch, a catering manager, who offers to help her find Lysaght. His outward affability conceals more sinister undertows and, stealing her meagre funds, he makes her heavily reliant on him. As her journey takes on nightmarish levels, Felicia becomes ever more adrift – yet eventually reaching a form of stability by the journey's end.

Historical Context

Writing in his non-fiction work *A Writer's Ireland: Landscape in Literature*, Trevor reveals his preoccupation with both the geographical and historical contours of the Irish landscape:

> In Ireland you can escape neither politics nor history, for when you travel through the country today the long conflict its landscape has known does not readily belong in the faraway past as Hastings or Stamford Bridge does for the English.[30]

This contrast between English and Irish landscapes becomes a significant symbolic theme in this novel as Felicia makes her journey through these two very different terrains. Capturing the banality of her small-town existence, Trevor also indicates some of the changes experienced in these places in the last decade of the twentieth century. Poised before the excesses of 'Celtic Tiger' Ireland, Felicia's home town resembles many Irish small towns, with its familiar buildings, businesses and institutions. In the book, as Felicia struggles in her quest in the alien landscape of industrial Britain, she consistently recalls her home town, its inhabitants and especially her friend Connie Jo's wedding, when she herself met Johnny Lysaght – 'the day has been special ever since'. Through her memories and dreams, we catch glimpses of her town:

> the sprawl of the convent at the top of steep St Joseph's Hill, and the Square with its statue of the gaitered soldier, and vegetables lank outside the shops in the summer heat. There was the chiming of the Angelus; turf smoke was pungent on the air. (*FJ*, p. 66)

Other landmarks include Hickey's Hotel on the Square, with its Kincora Lounge, a Coffee Dock, the Two-Screen Ritz and the Dancetime Disco.

Combining aural and visual aspects, Felicia's vivid recall of her home town has an intensity and focus. Trevor's familiarity with and visualisation of the Irish landscape, however, is not that of a romanticised or picturesque 'tourist gaze'. Rather, as he has noted, the ravages of the historical conflict have scarred the landscape and are not easily erased. The unfinished narrative of Irish history is written into its hills and valleys, in its monuments and ruins, in its small towns and rural townlands. His writing probes below the surfaces of the landscapes and towns, aware of their hidden stories and often unresolved histories. For Trevor, the commonplace and the small carry a narrative charge. He creates a sense of time and space in his fiction through his use of brand names and film titles – from the Centra store to the Bus Éireann logo with its elongated red setter (*FJ*, p. 39) or *Basic Instinct* being shown in the local cinema. As with other Trevor fiction, the past hovers in the present and suggests a sense of how slowly change came in rural Ireland (at least up until the major transformations of the mid-1990s).

The strong visual sensibility and the narrative charge characteristic of Trevor's fiction also finds echoes in the paintings of Martin Gale, who has been described as 'a faithful reporter of the rural Irish landscape'.[31] In his catalogue essay of 2004, S. B. Kennedy refers to the parallels between Gale's work and Trevor's fictional scapes, and the comparison is instructive. Gale's view of the land echoes Trevor's avoidance of the picturesque, although each in their distinctive medium evokes the place and changing spaces of rural Ireland. Gale's paintings are charged with narrative possibilities that echo Trevor's word-pictures.

The following paintings – their very titles suggesting stories and dramas – illustrate this shared ground of Trevor and Gale. In 'Cross Roads' (2003), no human figure is necessary to develop the sense of drama. Signposts and shadows, hedgerow and horizon have an Edward Hopper-esque quality of something about to happen. 'Bus Stop' (1981) (Plate 5) might serve as an illustration of Felicia's departure. On the side of an empty, rural road a young woman waits alone, her hold-all on the ground by her feet. In the foreground a discarded bicycle leans against a fence, and in the middle distance are agricultural buildings as the road gives way to the land and tall dark trees. 'By Pass 2' registers the changes wrought by recent Celtic Tiger prosperity as it cuts its way through the physical and social landscape, dramatising old and new, tradition and modernity, cottage and bungalow. Ribbon developments with incongruously grand names like Avalon or Shalamar, waterlogged tracks, rusted bangers, by-passes and church towers are all featured in Gale's landscape paintings.

As with Gale, Trevor's fictional landscapes are social spaces in which people live, work and struggle with the commonplace and the minor dramas. Gale's 'Madonna of the Fields', in which we see a young mother carrying her toddler, is a subtle coalescence of tradition and modernity as she walks through the field in sight of the town steeple. Recalling other rural Irish mothers whose stories did not have a happy ending (from teenager Anne Lovett dying in the shadow of a shrine to the case which came to be known as the Kerry Babies), Gale's and Trevor's refusal of the postcard culture allows a more sinewy engagement with time, space and change in Irish culture. Gale's realist paintings, charged with the clarity of pop-art, delineate details of different churches, barns, sheds, furrowed fields and ditches as well as the land of JCBs and SUVs, landscapes where the remnants of the past are not fully erased and not quite past. Similarly, Trevor's

Plate 5. 'Bus Stop', Martin Gale (1981)

world carries reminders of old pieties and tyrannies not yet finished. Hence, it is not the idealised 'tourist gaze' which frames these worlds, and which so frequently becomes part of the cinema's visual regime, but a more sober insight into the small realities of the banal and commonplace. Curiously, despite his eschewal of the romanticised iconography associated with the cinema – since the very earliest films made in Ireland – which becomes part of the tourist gaze and, in turn, reproduces and perpetuates it, Trevor's fictionalised Ireland retains its own currency and has been harnessed frequently for screen adaptation during the past three decades.[32]

The world depicted by Trevor in *Felicia's Journey* is far from the idyllic tourist scenery, and her meagre comforts and sober existence could belong to an earlier decade rather than late twentieth-century Ireland with its onslaught of crass consumption of a boom economy. His insistence on visual detail drives home the contrasts between Felicia's pre-Celtic-Tiger Ireland and her dislocation in post-Thatcherite Britain.

Felicia's Family Background and Situation

Trevor's fiction constantly explores how legacies and memories of the past inform and often unsettle the present lives of his characters. Often it is not so much a specific event as much as the social climate or social ecosystem developed in the fledgling Irish State, which had sought to establish a particular kind of nation underpinned by a form of both economic and cultural protectionism. The image of Ireland which was thus promulgated gained its most potent expression in Eamon de Valera's idealised vision, which he presented in his broadcast to the nation of 17 March 1943 on Radio Éireann, and in the specific roles identified in the 1937 Constitution of the Irish State (Bunreacht na hÉireann). The crucial touchstones of Felicia's household are those revered memories of the struggle for Irish freedom, the contribution by local heroes and the role of her great-grandmother, whose physical presence Felicia endures each day. Her father's collection of documents and photographs 'were a monument to the nation and a brave woman's due, a record of her sacrifice's worth' (*FJ*, p. 26).

In the evenings he regularly honoured those 'revolutionary times'. The sentiments of de Valera infuse her father's collection and memories. Trevor elegantly but incisively undercuts the idealism of de Valera's vision when he presents the sentiments formally in the novel:

> The Ireland which we have dreamed of would be the home of a people who valued material wealth only as the basis of right living, of a people who were satisfied with frugal comfort . . . the laughter of comely maidens . . . the home of a people living the life that God desires men should live.
> (*FJ*, p. 27)

Trevor then immediately reveals the barrenness of that rhetoric as Felicia's unemployed status is made clear since the permanent closure of the local meat factory. Other opportunities for work are remote in the locality. The ironies and contrasts between the ideal and the actual bristle in the novel. Now Felicia's role is as a servant to her father, brothers and great-grandmother: 'her freedom had been taken from her with the loss of her employment' (*FJ*, p. 23). Even her father, who is steadfast in his nationalist ideals, alludes to the increasing erosion of standards, manifested in the unpolished brass plates of the local professionals: 'Her father says it's the way the country's going, brass plates unpolished, a holy show to the world' (*FJ*, p. 31).

The tyranny of the memory of the great and gallant deeds of local rebels and, more significantly for Felicia, her great-grandmother are the sources of her inferiority and oppression. The lack of opportunity in the small town, the limited horizon of her drab environment, has left Felicia vulnerable to the overtures of the engaging but useless Johnny Lysaght. Her small happiness on the day she meets him highlights her grim existence, and yet that day too is tinged with a tawdriness which Trevor subtly introduces. He shows her ill at ease with her appearance as bridesmaid at her brother's wedding. Not for her the full colour blossoms of summer, but a 'bouquet of autumn flowers'. When the wedding party repairs to the hotel, we are aware of a shabby tinge to the place:

> Sister Benedict . . . was perched on the scarlet upholstery of a gold-painted chair, one of a set arrayed against the walls. The scarlet was soiled where it bulged, the gold of the legs worn away in patches, or chipped. (*FJ*, p. 16)

That Felicia succumbs to Johnny's dubious charms is not surprising given the grim existence she leads in her father's house. It is also not surprising that, when she finds herself with child, she leaves that house. As Dolores MacKenna suggests, Felicia is 'as isolated as any unmarried mother of the 1950s. The values which obtain in 1990s Ireland, as Trevor depicts them in this book, have not changed in over a century.'[33] The long shadow of the de Valera value system continues to persist and restrict Felicia's world, forcing her on her journey to England. Trevor sets up resonances with the 'Kerry Babies' case, to link Felicia's plight with other unwed mothers and their moments of crisis, which entered the public consciousness during the last decades of the twentieth century. It is also his means of reminding readers of the vexed and troubled history of Irish women's countless journeys to England to procure abortions as the Irish State persisted in its neglect and denial of real women's lives, in thrall to dated values and old pieties.

Felicia's own journey opens the novel. We accompany her on her boat journey across the Irish Sea and her train journey to England's industrial heartland. The complex narrative unfolds through a series of her memories, flashbacks and dreams as well as her diverse exchanges and encounters. Her boat journey precedes the jet-speed 'no-frills airline' culture now central to modern European travel. Then, as the train travels towards its destination, Trevor draws out the contrasts between Felicia's familiar Irish home and her heightened awareness of a foreign landscape: 'Later, there are long lines of motor cars creeping slowly on nearby roads . . . Pylons and aerials clutter a skyline, birds scavenge at a rubbish tip. There's never a stretch of empty countryside' (*FJ*, p. 5).

Her enforced emigration recalls the generations of Irish people who were forced into exile and emigration mainly through economic circumstances. Her situation is thrown into greater relief by her paltry luggage, making her visibly conspicuous. The novel builds up Felicia's isolation, leaving her again vulnerable to another man's overtures, this time Mr Hilditch. Her appearance and progress are noted by Hilditch, who immediately realises that 'she doesn't belong' (*FJ*, p. 11). Reinforcing the lack of belonging is the name 'Chawke's' and the Celtic patterns on her carrier bags, which are also out of place here. Trevor delineates the recessionary times of early 1990s Britain and conjures up a landscape which is grim, foreign and threatening to Felicia. Bewildered by the strange accents, she also struggles to negotiate the drab industrial estates with their 'endless repetition of nondescript commercial buildings' and their forest of trade-names and logos. Trevor, however, also introduces the legacy of industrial Britain; by invoking Dickensian England, he suggests an infernal atmosphere, reinforcing the sense of Felicia's cultural dislocation, uprooted from the familiar accents and contours of her Irish homeland with its comforting small-town familiarity, even if it entails traces of the 'mean and straggling towns' in George Russell's view. In Felicia's new landscape, 'Against a grey sky, tall bleak chimneys belch out their own hot clouds. Factories seem like fortresses . . . The lie of the land is lost beneath a weight of purpose, its natural idiosyncrasy stifled, contours pressed away' (*FJ*, p. 34).

Trevor's precise visual details emerge as a metaphor and dramatise Felicia's dislocation as he marks the contrasting registers of the English terrain, from the belching towers and the drab and repetitive roads of the industrial estates where 'nobody casually walks', to the streets where 'the picturesque [is] preserved as if in protest at the towers and chimneys which mar the town's approaches' (*FJ*, p. 35).

The endless roads, the patchy and flawed information about name changes and take-overs, indicate the futility of her search for Lysaght in this labyrinth of repetitive lines of commercial estates, where the land is artificially flattened and nobody walks along the roads. That Felicia has journeyed a long way from her father's house is clearly geographical in nature – the changes visible in topography and landscape – but it is also a huge social and cultural journey. Trevor depicts the irredentist rhetoric of her father and, in so doing, articulates the rigidity of the traditional, Catholic and rural identity which would neither admit nor allow for other ways of seeing or being. This identity evacuates any experiences that did not conform to the ideal, as they were erased from the official version of Irishness, so that Felicia, as an unwed mother, is forced into an emigrant's state of exile. Felicia's experience mirrors generations of other Irish people forced to emigrate, whose stories Trevor frequently imagines and reinstates in his fiction. As Fintan O'Toole asserts: 'The Irishness that was constructed by positing a Catholic, rural identity – and thus, of course excluding Belfast – was also one that could paint out emigrants.'[34]

Locating Mr Hilditch

If Dickens's influence informs Trevor's depiction of the industrial Midlands of England, Victorian influences are also detectable in the representation of Mr Hilditch. Trevor's approach is subtle, presenting the physically large presence of Hilditch, his small hands and delicate fingers, his frequent treats of chocolate bars and biscuits and his job as a catering manager, before he hints at darker, more hidden aspects of his character. His outward respectability and affability, Trevor informs us, conceal 'aspects of the depths that lie within him' (*FJ*, p. 7). Such double-sided natures have established legacies and origins in the 'sensation novels', where guilty secrets and family mysteries lurk behind the curtains of respectable middle-class society.[35]

While sensation novels retained the Gothic elements of the late eighteenth and early nineteenth centuries in their aim to generate fear in the reader, they resolutely avoided the typical Gothic settings of castles and monasteries, instead locating the fears and terror in familiar and contemporary settings. These elements inform the characterisation of Hilditch and are deployed to create a contemporary monster. In establishing Hilditch in this way, Trevor sets up a narrative agenda of suspense, alerting readers to Hilditch's potential menace. Dolores MacKenna identifies Trevor's use of the Gothic convention to explore themes of evil, guilt, madness and fantasy in much of his early work[36] and these are elaborated with precision in the figure of Hilditch. Again, Trevor's mode of address is to evoke Hilditch's personality through his home and possessions on a visual level. He takes time to describe in detail the large, detached house, built in 1867, which Hilditch occupies on his own and which he has inherited from his mother. In a reversal of the norm, Hilditch has sold all of his mother's furniture and made it 'solely his'. He achieved this by amassing his own collection of articles, which included:

> huge mahogany cupboards and chests, ivory trinkets for his mantelpieces, secondhand Indian carpets, and elaborately framed portraits of strangers. Twenty mezzotints of South African military scenes decorate the staircase wall, an umbrella-stand in marble and mahogany vies for pride of place with a set of antlers in a spacious hallway. (*FJ*, p. 13)

Although Hilditch confines his forays to local salesrooms, the objects which he chooses to adorn his house recall the British imperial legacy in faraway colonial exploits which brought home booty and established large collections – and the 'imperial archive' which is so central to empire from the nineteenth century onwards.[37] The colonial theme is reinforced in Hilditch's address: his road is named after the Duke of Wellington, the reluctant Irish-born soldier and administrator who moved up the Empire's hierarchy from India to the Peninsular War, and the victory at Waterloo to the heart of Westminster. Casting Hilditch in this way, Trevor spawns resonances whose metaphorical significance develops throughout the narrative. It also alerts us to Hilditch's penchant for fabrication, especially in terms of his own history and identity. Curiously, rather than retaining his mother's things, he replaces them with 'elaborately framed portraits of strangers', while the military images underscore his frustrated ambitions for a military career. Trevor's method in listing the objects in the collection recalls listed collections in a traditional museum; arguably, Hilditch's house is presented as a museum piece. With its 'ornate gas lamps, no longer in use', and shrubberies which he tends, 'though not growing anything new', it suggests Hilditch's predilection for living in the past with an ersatz history of his own construction.

His ties to the past are also carried through in his dislike of various aspects of contemporary life. In the novel he does not have a television, nor has he ever felt the need for a telephone, and he considers that 'there is so much violence in the world, so much prickliness' (*FJ*, p. 41), which he finds unattractive. The museum-like aspect of his house also owes something to the Gothic convention, where 'the shrubberies that shield the house from the street are dank and dripping on a misty morning' (*FJ*, p. 8), and is also central to the visual and cinematic representation which will be addressed later. Hilditch's identity is not only located within a form of arrested development: caught up in a past of his own making, the metaphorical extension of his museum-like dwelling also invests the narrative with a historical dimension. The museum was central in Victorian England. Indeed, the process of collecting and archiving knowledge from the far-flung colonies of the Empire was bound up with power and control of those distant terrains and cultures. Hilditch's domesticated version of the Victorian museum's colonial role reasserts its influence down through the decades to the late twentieth century, linking his predatory moves on Felicia with a history of colonisation, substantially emphasising the role of representation as a means of control and projection of the imperial gaze. Hilditch's consistent reference to Felicia as 'the Irish girl' underpins this attitude. And although Hilditch's paternal lineage is uncertain, through his collections and archive of portraits, objects and treasures, he attempts to imagine a plausible lineage and identity. The historical role of the archive is further domesticated and simultaneously horrifying as the contents of his own archive – called Memory Lane – are revealed. The narrative of colonial domination receives a further charge in the film adaptation when the girls are revealed in a taxonomy of races.

The Place of Food as a Signifier

Weighing a constant nineteen stone, Hilditch's job as a catering manager allows him to indulge in eating large meals and numerous snacks. The novel delights in describing different meals, whether those he is compelled to sample in his canteen or the various meals he consumes in different eateries throughout the story. Hilditch's enjoyment of food is eventually revealed as an obsession and, curiously, it is not an emphasis on the exotic so much as a reinforcement of the mundane and ordinary. His is not the gourmet palate: it is more the robust, even stodgy palette of the English kitchen, from his breakfast of bacon and eggs with 'toasted pieces of thick-cut Mother's Pride' (*FJ*, p. 8) to the 'casserole of beef' which he samples with 'potatoes, roasted and mashed, Brussels sprouts and parsnips' and 'raspberry-jam steamed pudding, the custard and apple crumble'. His shopping is also for everyday products:

> cod in batter, faggots, garden spears, broccoli spears, four bags of chips and two tubs of strawberry and vanilla ice-cream. In the fresh meat section, he picks out pork chops, chicken portions and prime steak . . . and bourbon creams, custard creams, lemon flakes, chocolate wafers and chocolate wholemeals . . . Since Mr Kipling's Bakewell Slices are reduced, as are Mr Kipling's French fancies and McVitie's treacle cake, he helps himself to a selection and to packets of jumbo-size crisps and Phileas Fogg croutons. (*FJ*, pp. 82–83)

Hilditch's regular choice of eateries such as the Happy Eater and Little Chef are a further insistence on his drab ordinariness. The novel deploys food as a signifier of his banal life and identity, but it is his obsessive interest in and consumption of food which also alerts us to his other side. Food, its preparation and consumption, takes on a more intense symbolic role in the film adaptation and explicitly links the role of nurture, food and mother in a domestic space. While Hilditch is seen using food to nurture and assist Felicia, it is also his method of entrapment. Through his apparent assistance he begins to consume her, taking over her time and her space and eventually taking control over her body when he persuades her to have an abortion.

A sense of his predatory hovering is frequently suggested, as he spends hours in his car, up and down the motorways. With Felicia, he is watchful and waits for her to reappear at bus stations and, asserting a wider reference to Anglo-Irish relations, he indicates Felicia's position through his aforementioned appellation 'the Irish girl' rather than allowing her the status of the other girls in his Memory Lane, whose names and memories he constantly evokes and draws to the surface, recalling their different encounters in different places, mainly cafés and eateries. That his encounter with Felicia has a different charge is signalled in his abandonment of his own rule – not soiling his own doorstep – as well as his chilling hint regarding the brevity of these relationships.

Memory Lane

A key to Hilditch's personality is his recourse to the gallery of memories and images which he calls his Memory Lane. In his encounter with Felicia, 'the Irish girl brings it all back' (*FJ*, p. 42). His recollections of the various girls and their locations are always there, which Trevor presents in cinematic terms – shadowy and dark 'until something occurs to turn its lights on', an image of Hilditch lying awake at night and waiting for 'the glitter to come'. There is a cinematic dreamlike quality to his Memory Lane as he conjures up the 'floating snapshots of Elsie and Beth and the others'. There is a curious blend of the commonplace with more lascivious and sinister dimensions in this Memory Lane. The locations for his encounters with the girls – places such as cafés and electrical showrooms – are juxtaposed with his memories, minutely and languorously detailed, of their bodies, their dress, their underclothes. In a direct allusion to Hollywood's legacy of *noir*-ish femmes, Hilditch recalls the characters in his Memory Lane as catalogued pictures in his private exhibition or gallery warehouse, each portrait with a name and a place: 'Elsie Covington had cropped up in Uttoxeter, Beth in Wolverhampton, Gaye in Market Drayton. Sharon was Wigston; Jakki, Walsall' (*FJ*, p. 51).

That he himself is vaguely aware of his darker side but intent on suppressing this awareness is explicit as he notes that 'certain things you don't even say to yourself, best left, best forgotten' (*FJ*, p. 42). Unlike the fabricated identity which he has constructed for himself in his house and hallway, where 'a stranger's gallery' of 'other families' ancestors regard him', the characters in his hidden Memory Lane/gallery/museum are his personal collection of memories and conquests/victims – closed and concealed, not for public access.

This recurrent trope of gallery/collection – both the ersatz and the interior memories – invites a comparison with the wider role of museum and gallery collections. Writing in *The Imperial Archive* (1993), Thomas Richards explores the role of the archive and various learned societies in constructing the idea of the Empire and, significantly, its representation in Victorian fiction. He notes the steady expansion of domestic institutions such as the British Museum into the colonial world through the collection and classification of information and data, ordering the empire into a manageable 'file-cabinet size'.[38] The drive to order and unify the data was seen as an easier task than ordering and maintaining direct physical control of these distant and scattered territories. Essentially, the imperial archive was a semi-myth of unity in an ideological project of the State and Empire. Hilditch's little collections, fragments of his own little empire, are a version in miniature of the imperial archive and, more significantly, are his attempts to construct a unified self and identity. His choice of objects, the gallery of strangers, these are his means of inventing an identity which unifies his fractured self – one both emotionally, sexually and psychically abused as well as disappointed in his sub-military ambitions. Attaching to himself remnants of the Empire and filling his house with the portraits of strangers, he attempts to suppress his real origins and circumstances, where he knows little of his father, is deluded in his potential by an uncle who is not one, and his mother who commits the ultimate transgression of boundaries. The collapse of the normal boundaries is inverted in Hilditch's drive for order as he fashions and curates a fantasy identity through his imperial bricolage. On a wider metaphorical level, the role of the British museum in Victorian culture, simulations of which adorn Hilditch's house, offers an example of 'the confluence of the aesthetic and political spheres of representation' as the colonial treasures are brought back home.[39]

The legacy of the imperial museum takes on a closer and more domestic layer when we note Hilditch's growing interest in 'the Irish girl' as we are shown how he obsessively stalks her. The fact that she comes from farther afield than any of the others in his gallery is a challenge, as is the fact that she is 'passing trade', adding a frisson to his anticipation. His history of preying on homeless girls gains additional edge with this Irish girl, whose wanderings have a nomadic dimension which he attempts to control – in like manner as the Empire/State had sought to categorise and control the nomadic flows of subjugated populations in the late nineteenth and early twentieth centuries. The nomadic represents a threat insofar as it represents flow – all that which cannot be contained, pinned down. Felicia, homeless and adrift, with child and from Britain's oldest colony, assumes allegorical significance with Hilditch's growing determination to control and contain her – and her fertility, through making her abort her child.[40]

4

NOVEL DEPARTURES

Egoyan imposed his own vision on Felicia's Journey, *producing a brilliant film, but one that diverges considerably from Trevor's text.* (Mary Fitzgerald-Hoyt, *William Trevor: Re-imagining Ireland,* 2003)[41]

The film adaptation of *Felicia's Journey* was directed by Atom Egoyan and released in 1999. While a central theme of popular discussions about adaptation is a consideration of the new work's 'fidelity' to the source material – in this case William Trevor's novel – several film scholars have indicated the limitations of this approach[42] and have pointed out more fruitful avenues of enquiry. David Lodge[43] has suggested that any consideration of a performance can generate different approaches and routes through a text. In a similar way to the evolution of the cover images of *Felicia's Journey* across different media, from the first-edition book cover to the cover image of the DVD issue, the process of transposition from the original source material to the film medium invites an exploration in terms of an evolutionary process, particularly as it applies to the images used to tell the story.

Narrative and Visual Style
The opening sequences of the film version of *Felicia's Journey* are rich examples of the potency of images in creating narrative atmosphere and entry points for viewers. On a black background, following the production company's logo, the film opens in Hilditch's house. In a dimly-lit interior, the camera moves very slowly and deliberately, with a childlike gaze, picking out objects and props, moving slowly upwards to present a glass case containing different specimens of eggs, hinting

at themes of fertility.[44] Ranging from exotic examples, the camera tilts upwards to a higher shelf to reveal domestic cardboard eggboxes and more familiar fare. Continuing its slow choreography, the camera finds other items – a glass decanter, a framed collection of insignia, other military memorabilia, toy ships, figurines, photographs. The camera moves around the rooms, catching a framed portrait of what will be revealed as Gala, Hilditch's mother, before entering the kitchen. Over these images, the credits of the film roll in a 'Dymo' typeface, prefiguring the Dymo labelling which Hilditch uses in his video archive, Memory Lane. The title, 'Felicia's Journey', contains a space error – a further indication of the amateur status of Hilditch's video collection? Or hinting, perhaps, at the one-chance nature of a Dymo lettering machine, which captures mistakes as well as the intended. These opening images are accompanied by the song 'The Heart of a Child', the highly sentimental lyrics aspiring towards a mythical childhood world. As the camera reaches the portrait of Gala, the music changes to a more romantic and schmaltzy theme, consisting of cascading Mantovani-like high strings, which will be reprised during the film and operate as a kind of leitmotif for Gala/mother. These opening images of Hilditch's domestic space present a home enveloped in an atmosphere of the past, whose decor and furniture carry a period feel and not the 1990s in which the story is set. The sense of a time-warp, which is also a feature of the novel, is further reinforced once the camera brings us into the kitchen, where Hilditch is preparing a meal. He stands before an elaborate *mise-en-place*, with a copper saucepan and decanter. Beside him on a domestic VCR and TV screen, Gala/mother is demonstrating a recipe and Hilditch slavishly tries to imitate her techniques and gestures as he prepares his meal. The celebrity chef programme in which she features is in black and white, further emphasising the past in this kitchen whose layout and decor also belong to another time.

Cut to the foam wake of a ship's journey, an overhead shot of a ship's deck and a young girl (Felicia) is visible as the boat leaves the coastline. A plaintive Irish melody accompanies these early images of Felicia. The film then cuts to Hilditch in a factory canteen kitchen, chatting to his staff and, as a reinforcement of his interest in food as indicated in the opening sequences, he is heard encouraging one of the cooks and insisting that everything should be just so: 'It starts with the stock. Don't rely on cubes.' Next the film turns to Felicia at a British port; perhaps, judging by the official's accent, she is in Wales. She is flustered and confused by the questions that the immigration officer asks her. Quite unprepared for international travel, Felicia has 'no documentation of any kind'. After a brief flashback – with her head nestling in the arms of Johnny Lysaght to the sound of church bells – she arrives in Birmingham. A slight figure, Felicia's dislocation and sense of strangeness becomes more evident when she reaches the city, her frail frame dwarfed by the buildings, the flyovers, the bustle and the people while the discordant strings on the soundtrack bring a tonal footnote to the visual metaphor.

In these opening sequences, the film presents two parallel narratives, opening on Hilditch (and quickly emphasising his conservative nature when a sales rep demonstrates a food vending machine) and then introducing Felicia, and suggesting a potential narrative link through the sequencing. There is a third narrative strand offered through Felicia's flashback, giving glimpses of her first encounter with Johnny Lysaght, the father of her unborn child, in search of whom she is making the journey. The juxtaposition of the diverse narrative strands – the story of Hilditch and Felicia, the narratives made available through their individual memories – is given a further layer of complexity with the video images of Gala's cookery programmes, the home movie footage and the more sinister video archive of 'talking heads' in Hilditch's Memory Lane.

The reflexive dimension inherent in the use of these contrasting visual styles is a feature of Egoyan's cinema. His characteristic use of home movie footage acts as an additional narrative agent. In this film, it works on several levels: along a hermeneutic axis, offering an enigmatic turn as to their significance in the story; on a reflexive level, posing questions to do with technology, media and individual memory; and at the level of pure cinema, using the different visual registers to provide narrative texture. The contrast between how Felicia's memories are rendered as cinematic flashback within the overall narrative and the ways in which Hilditch in his 1950s world has to rely on gritty modern video technology (or home movie footage) distinguishes their relationship to their pasts. Felicia is shown recalling the joy of her encounter with Johnny Lysaght as well as her failed exchanges with his possessive mother – all filmed and presented within the main film style. Likewise her memories of her leave-taking – her promises to her grandmother, her fraught conversations with her father – are all captured within the main visual register. Even when under anaesthetic towards the end of the film, her troubled state is expressed in strong visual terms, with images of Lysaght, their imagined child and her own father melding into each other as an idealised family portrait.

Hilditch's memories, however, are of a different register. His memories of his childhood are rendered in the style of a home movie. In the present, his theft of Felicia's meagre nest-egg triggers an earlier memory of stealing, brought on by his resentment of his mother's irritation with him as he disrupts her filming schedule. Memories of his mother and his relationship with her are also filtered through film – his childhood and his mother mediated both literally and metaphorically in the visual style of the film. In Trevor's novel, much of Hilditch's memories appear normal and almost innocuous before slipping into the darker recollections of failure and abuse. A telling moment in the novel occurs in the clinic where he has brought Felicia to have an abortion. Hilditch exposes his creepy excitement as he imagines how he is perceived by staff in the clinic – as the father of her unborn child – 'a relationship has occurred' (*FJ*, p. 136), which prompts him to think about his own mother. The ending of Felicia's motherhood is closely interwoven with Hilditch's memory of his own mother as he thinks: 'Funny if she were here now . . . funny if she came back from the dead' (*FJ*, p. 137). In the film, this is precisely what happens. Through his video technology, she is constantly present but ever distant. The complex blend of diverse visual styles enriches the hermeneutic strand, especially in the presentation of the video clips from Memory Lane and Hilditch's early use of his video camera's surveillance of Felicia when offering her a lift. It is a curious shot and presents a fragment of her body – her shoes, which, through the restricted angle, are all that the concealed camera can capture. Yet another fragmented image of Felicia, again from Hilditch's viewpoint, comes in her reflection in his side-view mirror, reminiscent of Hitchcock's rear-view image from the interior of Marion Crane's car in *Psycho*.

Landscape: Industrial Britain

The role of landscape and the sense of place in the novel functions not only on a geographical and topographical level but also on a metaphorical one. Felicia's journey from her small-town rural roots to the industrialised and urbanised English Midlands is also key in the visual style in the film. Her alienated experience at stations and factory gates is visually manifest through her dress and unsuitable shoes, which are inappropriate for her long journey and suggest that she expects to find Johnny Lysaght right away. These encumbrances amplify her feeling of strangeness and of 'being out of place' in the urban environment. The awkwardness of her movement, her apologetic and reticent gait, all go towards dramatising her sense of not belonging. There is an increased sense of this disorientation in Egoyan's use of the emblematic industrial landscape, which renders her insignificant in the frame. Giant redbrick cooling towers, vast steel structures, phalanxes of iron railings and Victorian gasometers frequently dominate the screen, invoking the overwhelming scale of the industrial sublime. All allude to the impact of the industrial revolution and echo the novel's Dickensian images – the factory interior where Hilditch works is a convulsion of noise, steam, smoke, drilling and frenetic activity. Outside, the frequent use of overhead and aerial shots to pick out the lone figure of Felicia on the canal tow-path or at the edge of a road junction as she makes her way through this landscape further visualises her dilemma.

Among the Ruins

The film's complex structure weaves present action with manifestations and portrayals of different memories and flashbacks. A consistent setting for Felicia's flashbacks is the ruins of an ancient church. The rupture between her rural homeground and the unfamiliar environment is frequently cued in visual contrasts but is also deftly carried on the soundtrack. Church bells signal a shift from the industrial grey to ecclesiastical grey stone of an ancient church in rural Ireland as Felicia remembers faith and fatherland. Working on several levels, it articulates her personal dilemma within her family circumstances – the law of her father made clear in his chastisement of her behaviour – but, shot within the ruins of the church, it is plaited with a legacy of nationalist and religious impositions to open onto wider questions of church laws, Irish traditions and local context. It also ferries into the text, through the setting of the father/daughter exchange, the history of how women and their bodies were difficult issues for the Roman Catholic Church even into the 1990s. In the film this remains underdeveloped, in contrast to the novel, which invokes recent events (such as the Kerry Babies case).[45] Situating several of the critical exchanges with her father among the ruins of an ancient church underpins her father's unquestioned commitment to a particular ideology and rhetoric. Caught up in his own history, he utters futile clichés – 'one day there'll be work for you' – and refuses to face any of the realities: that Felicia is no longer a child, that the small town offers little economic security. In a further flashback, Felicia and her father are shown as the small town closes in on their conversation, the father's sloganising rhythm echoing the visual constrictions in the scene.

The restrictions of small-town life are also key in another critical flashback as she recalls the unsatisfactory nature of Johnny Lysaght's departure – her eagerness to extend the moment interrupted by Johnny's motorcycling friend. Her efforts to make the leave-taking meaningful, to get a contact address, fail with the arrival of the bus to take him away. Trevor's novel also conveys her sadness and her reticence – 'not wanting to be pushy' in her request for an address – and her sick feeling as she watches him and his mother, 'her arm in his', taking Felicia's hopes away in the bus with 'an elongated red setter' on its side (*FJ*, p. 39). Shot against a background which includes the ancient ruins and framed by road signposts, Felicia and Johnny's goodbyes are hasty and humble. Aligned with ancient history and geographically embedded in local placenames and signposts (they are filmed here equidistant from Mitchelstown and Fermoy, while Ballindangan is closer), Felicia's future with Johnny is doomed, the ancient ruins a reminder of the burden of the past, the signposts a reminder of the present tenacity of small-town life and censure.

5

MOTHERLAND
·······································

> *When Mr Hilditch's mother died he sold her belongings to a clothes*
> *dealer.* (William Trevor, *Felicia's Journey*, 1994)[46]

Felicia's journey opens on the ferry to England. 'Taking the boat to England' is a phrase and image teeming with meaning for generations of Irish emigrants who for economic reasons sought work on the railways and roadworks, the hospitals and schools of 'the old enemy'. It has also been the route taken by many Irish women forced to seek legal abortions in England outside the tyranny of the Catholic Church and the Irish State, where abortion continues to be banned. Abortion is not Felicia's intention initially; her upbringing in rural Ireland, her treatment by her father and brothers, ensure that her motherhood outside of traditional marriage will not be tolerated. Nor will abortion be a later option, as Felicia imagines Father Kilgallen and Reverend Mother, 'both of them intent on preserving the life of the child that is her shame' (*FJ*, p. 69). Despite the idealisation of the mother role historically, emphasised in de Valera's vision which imbues Felicia's home, Trevor's representation of Felicia's situation undercuts any idealisation that may be propagated by Church and State. Felicia's own mother is dead. Like Bridie in Trevor's earlier story, 'The Ballroom of Romance', Felicia has lacked motherly nurture, instead catering to a great-grandmother, whom Trevor represents as 'Mother Ireland', an ideological and patriotic tyranny which, arguably, has prevented Irish women from realising and determining their own lives.[47]

If the myth of Mother Ireland hovers over Felicia and her journey, a more tangible and recent sense of the dangers of motherhood outside marriage in Ireland is laced through the novel through oblique allusions to the case of the 'Kerry Babies'. Trevor carefully plots allusions and images which echo the narrative of the Kerry Babies as a parallel to Felicia's dilemma. Felicia confesses her situation to Miss Furey, who was:

> middle-aged, unmarried, a woman to whom no man had been known to pay attention, yet about whom there had once been a rumour that she was pregnant. When abruptly her condition changed and she returned to normal it was said with certainty that no child existed in the farmhouse where she lived. (*FJ*, p. 56)

Hints of an incestuous relationship were rumoured, as well as an illegal abortion involving a Dublin chemist, and also a story 'claiming that the infant had been got rid of more crudely and been buried on the Fureys' land'. Later in Felicia's troubled dreams following the abortion, images tumble and collide into each other in her mind, and she imagines burying an infant under potato sacks, 'following him in the darkness and laying it down in the pit . . . and clay is shovelled in, the sods put back' (*FJ*, p. 143). The rural images of digging in the dark and burying a baby reverberate with the notorious media coverage of the Kerry Babies story, and the garda investigation. It also recalls an image from Hitchcock's 1972 film *Frenzy*, in which a female corpse is buried beneath potato sacks in a lorry.

Mother Ireland is also bound up with the image of the possessive mother of sons who will defend and protect her. Cathleen Ní Houlihan, the Poor Old Woman or the beautiful but entrapped women of the Aisling poetry of the eighteenth century, the potential of rescue and protection, all carried significant freight in patriotic culture.[48] But, arguably, this is also a form of tyranny in its possessive element. It is this possessive streak that characterises Mrs Lysaght, mother of the Johnny Lysaght who has impregnated Felicia and deserted her. Trevor describes Mrs Lysaght as 'bitter as a sloe' (*FJ*, p. 45) and her dogged determination not to assist Felicia in tracing him becomes palpable in her features as 'her mouth sagged, distaste crept into the coldness in her eyes' (*FJ*, p. 46) as she tells Felicia that 'you've had enough contact with him'. Seeing Felicia as a threat – like the other woman who had stolen her husband – Mrs Lysaght's motherly affection has been distorted into a destructive possession of her son, closed and trapped in her suspicion and bitterness. Echoing Lancy Butler's mother in 'Events at Drimaghleen', this possessive dimension of motherhood and its thwarted outcome unsettles the idealised picture of motherhood which informed both Catholic teaching and is enshrined in Article 41 of the 1937 Constitution of the Irish State: 'In particular, the State recognises that by her life in the home, woman gives to the state a support without which the common good cannot be achieved.'

Decades later, by the late 1980s and early 1990s (in which the novel is set), Felicia's lonely journey brings to the surface the tensions involved in such idealised notions and the situations of real women.

While we are offered only glancing references to Felicia's mother, who has been dead from early in her life, Trevor's novel also presents Hilditch's mother sparingly, in glimpses refracted through Hilditch's memories of her. To all appearances she is a single mother, although, with Uncle Wilf, her regular companion, she fuses her mother's role with a degree of teasing and flirtation, at times gently chastising her son and other times teasing his meekness. With a delight in romantic novels, her flighty nature is deftly indicated through references to various men: a policeman who helped release Hilditch's knee from the railings; the brush salesman who spread out his brushes for her; her brief encounter with a man in a train carriage, 'in the Longridge tunnel it was' (*FJ*, p. 194); an insurance man who winked; the barman at the Spa; Uncle Wilf, who was a regular visitor; and Joseph, who was 'just a beau' and whose first name is also Hilditch's. The boy's curiosity about his name is met with an almost parodic response, as his mother explains that he was called Ambrose after a name she found in a novel and which was also the name of a newsreader who, in addition to newscasting, was a cat burglar, 'which really caught [her] fancy' (*FJ*, p. 194). Trevor animates Hilditch's memories with resonances of normal childhood elements – the familiarity of the stairs where he cried and played with Dinky cars – contributing to the sense of normality which Hilditch invokes to dispel the menacing fantasies in his mind. As if to stop the narrative flow of his dark fantasies, 'like a film projected in a cinema', Hilditch turns over the pages of an old photo album, wherein are the conventional snapshots of an ordinary life – 'a plump child with a bucket and spade'. Safe in a cupboard are souvenirs of his childhood – the Dinky cars, a Meccano set, a Happy Families pack of cards (*FJ*, p. 191) – reinforcing one version of his life fuelled by one set of memories. However, just as Hilditch as an adult has projected a normal exterior, only to have this gradually revealed as a façade, these props and images of a normal childhood eventually give way to a darker reality.

Trevor's revelation of the incestuous core of the mother–son relationship is all the more shocking because of the stealthy way in which it is gradually unfolded for readers. Structured into a passage when he recalls events in his childhood, when he and his mother had watched *Dumbo* or *Bambi* together, he wonders if she had known that she would turn to him when her other lovers deserted her, when Uncle Wilf left and the policeman no longer called. The horror is reinforced in the juxtaposition of the homely details – the boy in his 'blue-striped pyjamas' woken up by a mother with a 'shred of tobacco on her teeth and a ginny breath' – overturning and contaminating the memories of the happy families image. The change in her is neatly suggested in Trevor's prose: 'Like a tattoo, she said, the lipstick on his shoulder. Her face was different then' (*FJ*, p. 195), and later there is evidence that it was ongoing, when she wheedles in her special voice, 'the promise that the request will never be made again, broken every time'. This contaminated history permeates the house, infecting his brighter recollections (of his school reports) and his aspirations for an army career, a house in Wiltshire – seeping forever into his memories, no longer retrievable. This polluted atmosphere provides some explanation for his expulsion of his mother's things from the house and his attempt to replace her presence with other people's portraits and memories. Accompanying all this is the knowledge of Uncle Wilf's treachery (when he finally realises Uncle Wilf's fabrication of an army family), the glory of a regimental career now reduced to Wilf's fancy for a 'bit on the side', until this too passed and mother and son are left on their own.

In the novel, Trevor offers a compelling image of Hilditch staring into a photograph of his mother, which he presents as an image of his imaginary deceased wife, Ada, and which fuses the identity of mother and (imaginary) wife, symbolically conflating sexual relations: 'He stares into his mother's face, blurred and misty in the photograph he has decorated with black crepe because he had to say this was his deceased wife. The eyes stare back at him . . .' (*FJ*, p. 193).

Hilditch and Hitchcock

The image in the photograph recalls another monstrous mother whose image and legacy continues to hover over popular culture. Mrs Bates in Hitchcock's 1960 film *Psycho* has become a central image of the Freudian anxiety in the relationship between mother and son. Norman Bates and his possessive mother occupy a brooding Victorian Gothic house and run the sinister motel in which the hapless fugitive, Marion Crane, finds her watery end. Both Bates and Hilditch share a crisis of identity and an inability to form sustained adult relationships. A key to their arrested development is the relationship with their mothers. Matrophobia, the fear of contact with the mother, troubles Hilditch, sinking under the weight of her will, subdued by her rasping ginny whisper. Haunting Hitchcock's work is the fear and threat of the devouring mother, mobilising male anxieties about identity, individuality and the fear of being swallowed up and annihilated.[49]

Drawing on the work of Julia Kristeva, Tania Modleski explores the notion of the feminine/maternal as a pollutant, because it undermines and subverts male symbolic systems and notions of identity and order – especially in capturing the symbolic swamping of Norman Bates's sense of self as he reacts by murdering a young woman, then carefully cleaning the bathroom, removing all traces of her blood and depositing her body in a car and burying it in a swamp. That Norman Bates shares with Hilditch a desire to clean and purge their houses of the female traces/DNA is manifested in the structure of Trevor's prose. Following recollected glimpses into his mother's promiscuity is an extended paragraph describing in detail his cleaning regime, which helps keep his more fearful thoughts and memories at bay: 'He cleans the room with his Electrolux and the hall and stairs, and his bedroom. He mops the vinyl of the bathroom and the lavatory, and scents the air with a herbal fragrance' (*FJ*, p. 194). And again, following a vivid memory of her abusive invasion, comes further cleaning and scouring of pans and surfaces. But despite his energetic cleaning activity, the memory surfaces of her scented powder, which 'clogged the pores on the two sides of her nose, a shade of apricot' (*FJ*, p. 195), polluting his memory, imprisoning him in it and retarding his development as an adult, sharing with other fictional serial killers this fear of the mother.

6

PSYCHO KILLERS:
HITCHCOCK, GENRE AND *FELICIA'S JOURNEY*

This is a thriller lifted to the level of high art. (Anon., *Publisher's Weekly*, 1994)[50]

When first published in 1994, several reviewers referred to Trevor's novel as a 'thriller' and considered it as something of a departure for the author. Yet, as Mary Fitzgerald-Hoyt points out, Trevor 'had a lifelong fascination with the thriller'.[51] Weaving crime fiction with an exploration of identity and psychological motivation, Trevor's novel was seen as combining conventions of a popular cultural form with serious literature. Crime fiction's durability as a genre and fluidity as a form is, according to Michael Dibdin,[52] a key to why serious writers often undertake to renovate its fields of possibility: 'the fact that crime writing is a distinctive genre, with flexible but fixed parameters and a limited repertoire of themes, has tempted so many mainstream writers to indulge in acts of homage, pastiche or cross reference'.[53]

Further evidence of the genre's currency comes from T. S. Eliot, who identified readers' pleasure in the thriller dimension of crime fiction: 'Those who have lived before such terms as "highbrow fiction", "thrillers" and "detective fiction" were invented realise that melodrama is perennial and that the craving for it is perennial and must be satisfied . . . and that the best novels were thrilling.'[54]

The social and cultural nuances which crime fiction articulates within the periods in which they are set (and produced) are also a source of their enduring potency, as writers continue to graft contemporary reflections onto the older form. The history of crime fiction bristles with such emphases, including the novels of P. D. James, Ruth Rendell and Colin Dexter – a history which is also characterised by shifts between detection and an analysis of the crime and the criminal identity.[55] The sinewy narrative textures, a feature of much crime writing, which invite reader and writer engagement are also central to the cinema of Alfred Hitchcock.

Hitchcock's influence was cited in several reviews, and publishers used this to promote later editions of the novel as well as locating it alongside contemporary doyens of the genre – 'A page-turner that will magnetise fans of Hitchcock and of Ruth Rendell'[56] – and Hitchcock's narrative strategies are detectable in Trevor's finely wrought story. It is also tempting to feel his influence in Trevor's novel, which, although actually describing Hilditch, recalls the famous silhouette of the 'master of suspense': 'His ponderous form is lit in the open doorway' (*FJ*, p. 197).

Hitchock's capacity for mobilising and generating suspense and his penchant for penetrating the darker corners of humanity are palpable too in Trevor's writing. While locating *Felicia's Journey* in a generic field invoking Rendell and Hitchcock, it is also clear that Trevor extends the contours of that genre to sift and investigate the human psyche and criminal impulses.

Echoes of Hitchcockian strategies emerge in the novel, drawing readers into an atmosphere of unease through deftly controlled narrative moments and scenes. In the novel, anticipation and anxiety are carefully built up, the alternating narrative voices (of Felicia at one time, of Hilditch at another) adding a complex texture to the story as it unfolds, building up the significance of objects, settings and exchanges and developing an unease as our sense of security seeps away and Hilditch's potential evil is revealed. The power of an otherwise banal event is captured here when we are shown an 'image of the green hump-backed car' (*FJ*, p. 20), alerting readers to a potential threat to Felicia who remains innocent of the menace awaiting her.

A further Hitchcockian flavour which demonstrates the powerful menace that can be created in the world of ordinary objects comes when Hilditch, making a hot drink for Felicia, recalls other similar banal objects which were eventually revealed as harmful and sinister: 'He pours the milk he has heated into two plain white mugs' (*FJ*, p. 134).

In 2001 the Pompidou Centre in Paris mounted an exhibition entitled 'Fatal Coincidences: Hitchcock and Art'. In a large-scale show, one room consisted of a darkened room filled with a series of vitrines containing the signature objects from Hitchcock's films. Metonymically charged, wrenched from their narrative flow, they sustain their power, creating an iconography which recalls but also goes beyond their specific narrative contexts. So Marnie's stuffed handbag, the glistening cigarette lighter and the glass of milk resonate with unease and anxiety.[57] The glass of milk which is carried upstairs in *Suspicion* (1941) and consumed in *Spellbound* (1944) makes its highly charged reappearance fifty-four years later in *Felicia's Journey*, appropriately at night-time and under the guise of nurture and kindness.

Just as objects have ferried sinister potential across Hitchcock's cinema and extended into other media narratives, the image of the isolated house also belongs to that world. The haunted house, long part of a Gothic tradition, is also a staple of much of Hitchcock's output and continues to exert a fear and fascination. Hilditch's house, though not approaching the grandeur of du Maurier/Hitchcock's Manderley, nevertheless resonates with those darker tones. His home at 3 Duke of Wellington Road is large and detached, 'built in 1867 ... it spreads from this lofty entrance hall to kitchen and pantries at the back' and 'the shrubberies that shield the house from the street are dank and dripping on a misty morning'. Its museum-like interior and atmosphere echoes something of the quality of Manderley as well as calling up memories of the Bateses' house on the hill behind their motel with all its secrets. These houses creak under the freight of the past – of memories, victims, rejection and psychological abuse. If Manderley is a psychological prison,[58] 3 Duke of Wellington Road is also a prison for Hilditch and eventually for

Felicia, the woman who knows too much, but who manages to escape its horrors. Just as Norman Bates is caught up in his past, Hilditch's house suggests a certain arrested development – a house without a telephone but with a gramophone, a room in which two grandfather clocks mark time in a time-warped space – all objects which are 'at peace with one another and have a meaning for him' (*FJ*, p. 150).

Different recollections hover in the house – Dinky toy memories, but also the memory of rejection, of his mother's cruel teasing, of Uncle Wilf's military stories and of Hilditch's rejection by the army – spawning a resentment which has grown in scale and imprisoned him over time. The careful preservation of the eponymous Rebecca's clothes in Manderley finds echoes in Hilditch's fabricated wardrobe for an imaginary invalid wife, Ada – part of the elaborate deception he creates to ensnare Felicia. It is not only the clothes which indicate his meticulous and obsessive commitment to detail. This is carried further in the way he arranges the space of her dressing table, emptying bottles of perfume and lotions until they are half full, to create a sense of a normal life. This is the forensic reconstruction of imaginary life-stories. Like Hitchcock's monsters, who are rooted in ordinariness and normality, Hilditch fuses his deceptions with the small details of an ordinary life. Just as Norman Bates initially appears to conduct a very ordinary conversation about stuffed birds – again the museum theme – with Marion Crane in the Bates motel, Hilditch's outward affability and his dedicated efforts in projecting the normality of his life with his imaginary wife Ada simply underlines the increasing extremes of his delusion and madness. While Norman Bates's voyeuristic impulse, underlined by the painting of Susanna and the Elders which conceals Norman's spyhole, is confined to the motel space, Hilditch's stalking is mobile and dynamic, unrestricted by walls and interiors as he waits and hunts for 'the Irish girl' at bus stations and street junctions. Hilditch's house, the Bates motel and house and Manderley also share a heightened sense of theatre, of scenes staged with props and objects to animate the delusions and imaginary worlds of their inhabitants: Mrs Danvers, orchestrating grand operatic finales – eternally committed to Rebecca; Norman Bates, with his museum of stuffed birds and a theatrical projection of his relationship with his dead mother; and Hilditch's own domestic museum of colonial conquests, almost entirely constructed out of other people's worlds.

Trevor's writing also shares with Hitchcock's approach the creation of suspense and the gradual release of the knowledge of the serial killer's madness and menace. Deploying familiar conventions of crime fiction, Trevor invokes the frisson of the genre. Just as Hitchcock's objects have over time accrued to themselves a sinister chill, Trevor is keenly aware of the value of conventions in engaging readers' expectation while also extending in different directions. Highly visual, Trevor's phrases draw on their generic history while avoiding any specific reference, their textual value being their generic recall. So Hilditch worries about 'shadows on the glass' and her 'eyes in the driving mirror'; and although they have been deployed in a specific narrative context, their generic echoes resonate within a decidedly cinematic legacy. Trevor's deployment of the hermeneutic code, in which readers are drawn into the fictional world to ponder what has happened to Felicia, echoes the central drive of much crime fiction. It is compounded by further anxiety as Trevor has gradually hinted at the fate of the other girls of Hilditch's Memory Lane. The growing sense of fear is underpinned by Felicia's realisation of what Hilditch is and has done. She registers his weight on the bed as he invades her disturbed dreams: 'an urgent throatiness only inches from her face', where 'no light comes from the window' (*FJ*, p. 153). Having carefully choreographed fear and unease, there comes a chilling short sentence: 'She knew the girls were dead' (*FJ*, p. 155). With Gothic echoes, the manner of the writing harks back to those other creatures of the dark: 'He has waited for the night to come and settle: the dark is what he chooses' (*FJ*, p. 155).

Trevor is also daring in allowing his central character to depart from the narrative at the end of chapter 19, deftly building the chilling fear and anxiety of the thriller genre as Felicia makes her exit from Hilditch's house:

> Cautiously, she steps out on to the landing, still gripping the bar of the grate, her two carrier bags slung from the crook of her free arm, her handbag looped about her body. She descends the unlit stairway, pausing every two or three steps to listen in case he has returned to the house. The metal bar makes a clatter on the tiles of the hall when it slips from her fingers. In a panic because she can't find the latch of the hall door, she feels for a light switch. (*FJ*, p. 156)

Serving as a suitable cliffhanger of panic in the darkness, Trevor then opens the following chapter in daylight and displaces the focus from Felicia to Hilditch, alone, as he visits a stately home. As a serial killer, Hilditch parallels the narrative role of Hitchcock's Uncle Charlie in *Shadow of a Doubt* (1943). As Charlie collects and refreshes his catalogue of conquests of merry widows, Hilditch has his Memory Lane, which he also renews.

Locating *Felicia's Journey* within the serial killer genre became a selling point for the film/video version. The cover of one video edition declaims 'Monsters are not born', while an extract from the *Sun* newspaper asserts: 'A mesmorising psycho thriller.' Hilditch, as a serial killer at the centre of the narrative, shares some of the characteristics associated with this generic role. Jane Caputi has identified typical elements of the serial killer,[59] particularly where the mother is often blamed for her son's criminality as a result of psychological or physical abuse. Obsession with the mother also characterises serial killer Jame Gumb, in Thomas Harris's novel *The Silence of the Lambs* (1988). Gumb shares with Atom Egoyan's Hilditch an obsession with watching his mother (now dead) on videotape, replaying a tape of her participation in a beauty contest as a prelude to another killing. He watches: 'And here she came, approaching the stairs in her white swimsuit, with a radiant smile for the young man who assisted her at the stairs, then a quick turn on her high heels, away, the camera following the backs of her thighs; Mom. There was Mom.'[60]

While the 'bad mother' is at the core of Trevor's novel, Egoyan, considering it in some way reductive, shifts the emphasis from the more conventional narrative manifestations of the serial killer form by according a more ambivalent dimension to the mother's role in creating Gala.[61] Norman Bates's skeletal Mom in the basement has become a ghost in Hilditch's video machine.

7

THE RAW AND THE COOKED:
FOOD, HILDITCH AND FILM
....

Food must be served by caring hands. It makes us feel loved.
(William Trevor, *Felicia's Journey*, 1999)

Food has been a compelling metaphor in literature and film, communicating social and cultural meanings. Roland Barthes in *Mythologies*, his collection of essays decoding aspects of 'everyday' life in France in the 1950s, explores several foodstuffs ('Steak and Chips') for their symbolic charge. Pierre Bourdieu, too, notes how food can signify social position; and anthropology, in work such as that of Levi-Strauss and Mary Douglas, has scrutinised the structure and cultural significance of cooking and eating.[62] In *Purity and Danger*[63] Douglas examines the meaning of pollution in relation to eating systems, and notes that formlessness is central to notions of pollution and contamination. Popular film continues to draw on the metaphorical currency of food, using the family dinner table as a setting rife with tension (for example, the repeated scene of the evening meal in Lester Burnham's home in *American Beauty*, the use of family dining in *The Sopranos*, or the communal commitment to preparing a good pasta sauce despite the confines of prison in *Goodfellas*).[64]

In Trevor's novel, the large and rotund figure of Joseph Ambrose Hilditch is established in his nineteen-stone bulk and his everyday activities which revolve around food – in his professional role as a catering manager and also in his consistent interest in food, as his shopping indicates, as well as in his various visits to different 'greasy spoons' and service cafés. Curiously, although Trevor in the novel notes 'how people from Pakistan and the West Indies have begun to

4

4

settle, changing the look of things' (*FJ*, p. 65), and despite the fact that Birmingham and the English Midlands where the story is set have become popularised alongside the likes of Bradford as the British home of curry and balti houses, Hilditch's diet remains trapped in a 1950s version of English cooking, even though ethnic restaurants had been a feature of Britain since the 1920s, 'serving nostalgic old colonials upon their retirement',[65] and popularised on the high street from the 1960s. Hilditch is aware of this too. He visits 'neighbourhoods the Indians or Pakistanis have taken over. The Boroda Express offers the variety stars of India: Bhangra Garta, Miss Bhavana, Deepa the voice of Lata. The Koh-I-Noor Restaurant is under new management' (*FJ*, p. 179). In the novel, it is also clear that Hilditch chooses his cafés/restaurants as his own theatre or stage set, where he can enact fantasies in full view of an audience (waitresses and receptionists, for example), through whose surveillance his fantasies gain structure and narrative depth.

Egoyan's film adaptation transposes the food theme in several ways. While losing the novel's frequent encounters in cafés, the film expands the food theme through visualising Hilditch in his catering role and, significantly, in the creation of Gala, a 1950s TV celebrity chef, as Hilditch's mother – in a powerful symbolic merging of food, nourishment and the maternal figure.

Drawing on the source novel's presentation of Hilditch's supervisory role in the factory canteen, the film presents scenes which dramatise and locate Hilditch's identity among his staff and fellow workers, underlining the importance of food in his life, both as a source of nutrition and as a spiritual and emotional comfort. When he advises one of his staff in an early scene, we can detect how food and its preparation are core aspects of his emotional world: 'food must be served by caring hands – it makes us feel loved'. This latter assertion is at the core of his dismissal of a salesman attempting to persuade him to install a vending machine which would provide food 'piping hot, or chilled or anything in between'.

The significance of food preparation is expanded further as the camera presents his elaborate preparations for an evening meal – in contrast to his reliance on café fare and convenience foods in the novel. The role of food as a central defining feature of his identity in the novel is explored for all its metaphorical aspects in Egoyan's film. Central to Hilditch's nightly culinary activities is the replay of Gala's (his mother) TV food programmes. These form the basis of Hilditch's culinary rituals. We can see that he is clearly a far more natural and adept cook than Gala. Yet in his attempts to imitate her gestures, carefully and obsessively watching her performances on video, recreating her meals, something is lost. It is his vain attempt to secure comfort and emotional contact with his mother. Endlessly replaying her meals; endlessly denied contact; endlessly experiencing the distance.

The maternal as the source of emotional and physical nourishment is here pursued endlessly but is also negated by the perversion of the maternal, as the novel indicates. The mother in the novel, who makes a travesty of the maternal role through her invasion of her son's bed, is transformed in the film into another kind of travesty. Gala performs her extravagant flirtation under the gaze of the camera's surveillance, performing a role for the camera in the kitchen where now, years later, Hilditch continues to watch her. Whether in the domestic setting or workplace, the kitchen as a site of meaning and identity for Hilditch is prime. The kitchen, which was Gala's main domain, calls up another relationship between Gala, food and Hilditch. It is shown to be the site of Hilditch's troubled childhood, his consequent identity turmoil and thwarted maturity. If stable identity and psychological maturity are established through clearly defined boundaries, it is clear in the novel and film that Joey/Hilditch's experiences of limits and boundaries are heavily troubled areas. It is through the symbolic nature of food that the issue of boundaries emerges as a subtext, particularly in the film.

As the anthropological work of Levi-Strauss and Mary Douglas indicates, the preparation of food and the arrangement of the domestic space are seen as a key site for the establishment and maintenance of appropriate boundaries, thus avoiding dirt and the danger of contamination. This offers insight into Hilditch's rituals and activities. His concern with cleanliness (both in the novel and in the film), his fastidiousness and attention to order can be seen, in part, as his attempts to avoid a breakdown of order with this associated dirt which the feminine/mother implies. The link between food and the body is also elaborated in the film, drawing on the messiness and viscerality associated with the physical body. Gala barely disguises her irritation and frustration with Joey's presence on and off screen and in a crucial scene forces him to ingest/swallow a piece of raw liver. In this narrative moment, the symbolic significance of food – especially, in this case, raw liver – brings together all of Joey/Hilditch's anxieties and fears of invasion and contamination. As Margaret Visser suggests: 'We hate whatever oozes, slithers and wobbles.'[66]

An explanation for this disgust is also stated in the work of Deborah Lupton, whose analysis draws on the theories of both Douglas and Julia Kristeva:

> Substances [such as liver] are too redolent of bodily fluids deemed polluting, such as saliva, semen, faeces, pus, phlegm and vomit. Such bodily fluids create anxiety because of the threat they pose to self-integrity and autonomy. Body fluids threaten to engulf, to defile, they are difficult to be rid of.[67]

This appears to be the complete inverse of the culinary obsessions of cinema's most famous serial killer, Hannibal Lecter, who happily 'ate his liver with some fava beans and a nice Chianti'.[68]

The trajectory of Egoyan's film, in this way, moves from an image of food in its nourishing capacity (prepared by caring hands) to one of food as an invasion and contamination. This narrative flashback pulls to the surface all the disgust that Joey/Hilditch experienced in his childhood, through his mother's excess. In this context, the nature of the maternal and, in a wider sense, the nature of woman emerges in the narrative. In her provocative study of Hitchcock's films, Tania

Modleski explores recurrent concerns in his work and how they are related to an ambivalence and anxiety about woman.[69] Revisiting the work of Levi-Strauss, in which male fears about annihilation and absorption by the female are delineated (and the related aspect of consuming and ingesting), she identifies in Hitchcock's films the image of the 'devouring mother', most dramatically sustained in the role of Mrs Bates (an image which is also explicitly recalled in Trevor's novel). Arguably, Hilditch's fear of his mother's dominant personality and her excessive sexuality prompted his efforts to expel her from the house – clearing it of all her possessions. Writing of the 'devouring mother', Modleksi clarifies: 'By "voracious", I refer to the continual threat of annihilation, of swallowing up, the mother poses to the personality and identity of the protagonists.'[70]

In his novel, Trevor suggests the sense of her invasive 'ginny breath' enveloping the young Hilditch. In the film, the creation of Gala poses the maternal excess in more visual terms. Julia Kristeva, in her study of horror, has explored the meanings of horror and phobia and argues that all are linked to matrophobia and relate to the fear of contact with the mother:

> that of being swamped by the dual relationship, thereby risking the loss not of a part (castration) but of the totality of his living being. The function of these religious rituals is to ward off the subject's fear of his very own identity sinking irretrievably into the mother.[71]

Kristeva's explorations of horror and rituals of defilement and the association of women as a 'pollutant' (following the work of Mary Douglas, whose analysis of boundaries and order is also illuminating in the context of Hilditch's actions) offer a way of linking Hilditch's obsession with food – its preparation and consumption – with his anxieties about his mother, his origins and his fractured self. Modleski, in her extended discussion of Kristeva's analysis of horror, asserts that, 'according to Kristeva, dietary prohibitions are based upon the prohibition of incest . . . and thus are part of the "project of separation" from the female body'.

As the novel makes clear, this separation for Hilditch was not permitted or achieved. Both Kristeva and Douglas note the 'unclean and improper coalescence' when boundaries are unclear. Fear and anxiety at the collapse of boundaries are seen as leading to rituals of defilement – for instance, the serial killing of different young women in an attempt to rid himself of the feminine and an attempt to re-establish order (often through ritualistic cleaning, as in *Psycho*) becomes Hilditch's fate. That he fears the physicality of the female body is clear in the novel and in the film. But the film, perhaps echoing Hitchcock, suggests a certain ambivalence – characterised both by desire for the female/mother and by a fear, even loathing, of the physicality that the female body represents.[72] This emerges clearly in the film when, after her abortion, we glimpse Felicia's blood-stained nightdress, or in the novel when Hilditch sees the contours of her body beneath her flimsy clothing.

Egoyan's characteristic use of different media is also pressed into play here. A TV set in the hospital reception (which Hilditch visits to add substance to the lie about his ailing wife) shows Rita Hayworth as Salome, presenting a severed head on a platter – combining subcurrents of the fatal female, devouring and all-consuming. It is an image which underlines Hilditch's thwarted psychology: revering – yet fearing – his mother, fantasising about paternity (yet persuading Felicia to abort her child). The emphasis on food as a signifier, in both the novel and the film, presents a rich and sometimes even humorous current: for example, in the novel, the extended inventory of Hilditch's shopping trolley; and in the film, Egoyan's creation of a 1950s television chef, a French-accented, post-war Nigella Lawson with shades of Fanny Craddock. At the same time, however, these carry darker symbolic freight and draw our attention to the ways through which Hilditch uses rituals to repress the more brutal sub-themes of consumption, as well as implying his fear of the viscerality in human relations.

8

'YOU BELONG TO ME':
POPULAR SONG IN *FELICIA'S JOURNEY*

It was the nature of the songs which interested me. Their sweetness,
their banality, their sugariness – you can almost lick them they
are so sweet, and yet they have this tremendous evocative power –
a power which is much more than nostalgia . . . They seemed to
represent the same kinds of things that the psalms and fairy-tales
represented: that is, the most generalized human dreams, that the
world should be perfect, beautiful and loving and all of those
things. (Dennis Potter, *Evening Standard*, 1998)[73]

In keeping with a character heavily attached to his Memory Lane,
Hilditch's choice of music reflects his obsession with the past. In the
novel, Trevor lists the titles of popular songs from the 1930s, 1940s
and 1950s, to indicate the period quality of Hilditch's musical taste
with which he fills his house, his world. But the song titles also
perform an additional narrative function, expressing the gap between
the lighthearted rhythms and lyrics of the songs and the darker aspect
of his character. They provide a musical equivalence to the
Jekyll/Hyde persona to which Trevor has already alerted us. Varying
in their musical styles – jaunty in some instances, such as 'Chattanooga
Choo Choo', or the excessively syrupy 'Charmaine' – his musical
selections are also often an extension of his interior fantasies.

While Felicia is recovering after the abortion, he puts on 'Besame
Mucho', 'and leaves the door open so that the melody can spread
through the house' (*FJ*, p. 147). He then sets about making two cups
of Ovaltine, later changing the record to 'Five Foot Two, Eyes of
Blue' and 'the music is soft enough to permit their conversation' (*FJ*,
p. 147). Later, however, as 'his memory flows destructively, the debris

of recall seeming more like splinters from forgotten nightmares' (*FJ*, p. 188) when the reality of his life begins to seep in, he uses the sweet strains of these popular songs in a vain attempt to comfort himself and to dispel the torrent of fearful memories that come after Felicia has gone and his appetite has vanished.

Citing titles of popular songs in the novel as a means of delineating character and interior mental states became problematic in the translation to film. The process of adaptation, in this context, offers an instructive insight into the financial dimension of the production process and helps to illuminate both the industrial and aesthetic aspects of film production. As Egoyan notes:

> In the script it was Peggy Lee, but because of the limitations of budget, we just couldn't afford it. One of the drivers listens to older songs all the time and I asked him if he could think of a singer Hilditch might listen to. He came back a couple of days later with this completely forgotten English singer from the 50s . . . called Malcolm Vaughan. He's hardly remembered but the songs are brilliant. And they're painful. So we've woven him into our film.[74]

The song 'Through the Eyes of the Child', which is used in the early scenes of the film, offers a musical anchorage to that narrative opening and reinforces the period atmosphere in Hilditch's house. At times signposting and underlining emotion, at other times signalling Felicia's homeland through Irish melodies and laments, the role of the soundtrack performs several narrative functions. Kate Bush's 'The Sensual World' hovers over the scene showing Felicia in the pub with Johnny Lysaght as an aural footnote to the action. For Hilditch, in the film as in the source novel, the popular songs with their banal lyrics are a significant part of his fantasy world (almost like a personal soundtrack for his life), providing musical extensions of his interior mental state or easing his pain. While incidental music generally plays an unobtrusive role in cinema, the very act of selecting popular songs for a soundtrack foregrounds their role in the piece. Egoyan has referred to the way in which he wanted to make the music 'a really active participant in the piece' and of how he wanted to 'use this music in a much more expressionistic way'. And while, conventionally, music may be used to reinforce emotion, it can also be used in a counterpoint fashion and he cites the way in which in *Felicia's Journey*, eventually, the sentimental strings soundtrack 'turns against' Hilditch.

Intertextualities

As with all adaptation, there is a strong intertextual dimension when source details are transposed and inflected in the new version, particularly in the use of popular songs. There is, however, an additional intertextual nuance in the film in the casting of Bob Hoskins in the role of the song-loving Hilditch. Hoskins also played the part of Arthur Parker, a travelling song-sheet salesman, in Dennis Potter's innovative six-part television series *Pennies From Heaven* (1978). Potter's acclaimed work for television is characterised by his innovative and overt use of popular song in drama. Arthur creates a fantasy romantic world through the words of the songs, asking his wife in one exchange: 'Don't you ever listen to the words in these songs?' But she dampens his fantasies, replying: 'That's not real life.' As Potter has argued: 'No matter how cheap, or banal or syrupy-syncopated they were, they were saying the world is better than it is. The world is a better place.'

It is this role that the songs frequently perform for Hilditch – drowning out his fears and anxieties, allowing him to enter his fantasies. In some ways, Potter's earlier experiment of 1967 with popular song as a narrative expansion, *Moonlight on the Highway*, about a deeply disturbed man who finds refuge and consolation in his obsession with the singer Al Bowly, anticipates the complex character of Hilditch. Hoskins's performance as the genial and timid Arthur, as well as his role in Neil Jordan's 1986 film *Mona Lisa*, indicates the rich intertextual currency of popular culture.

The music associated with the final images of *Felicia's Journey* echoes Felicia's Irish identity. Choosing a song in Irish, the language of her great-grandmother, its lyrics describe a love story and a sense of renewal that comes from the natural cyclical harmony of the seasons: 'Tiocfaidh an samhradh agus fasfaidh an fear' (The summer will come and the grass will grow).[75] Yet while the song opens with images of cyclical growth and renewal, nevertheless it is a ballad of unrequited love, striking an ambivalent note as the final lines point to the loss of sanity involved in this kind of love.

As MacKenna[76] demonstrates, the image of the garden as a place of hope is a consistent trope in Trevor's fiction, providing an earthly equivalence of Eden. In this context, we can read the film's images of growth and potential in tandem with the accompanying song as prompted by wider themes of renewal and compassion of the source novel.

9

MEMORY TEXTS

Reflection, projection and introjection . . . may create ambiguities about what is happening on the screen . . . Such narrative ambiguity recreates and expresses the ambivalent subjectivity and hybridised identity of exilic and diasporic conditions. (Hamid Naficy, 'Epistolarity and Textuality', 2004)[77]

Atom Egoyan's authorial concerns and themes are palpable across his cinema. From those which he developed as his original projects through to his adaptations, certain recurrent motifs and preoccupations emerge. While the themes and psychological concerns are played out across the different narrative structures, the process of his narration, his concern with ways of seeing and of telling through different mediating technologies, is a central force in his cinema: 'With my films, I'm interested in showing the frame as well as the picture.'[78] *Felicia's Journey*, although originating in a different field and context than his previous work, articulates some of Egoyan's recurrent explorations, such as dislocation, displacement and motivation. He shares with William Trevor the acuity of insight that is often the experience and position of the outsider. In adapting Trevor's novel for the screen, he relished the potential that the process of adaptation can offer for reworking the substance of the novel: 'There was . . . a sense of a moral universe I felt I could learn from.'[79]

Felicia's Journey, which deals almost exclusively with only two central characters, is nevertheless a complex narrative presenting distinctive narrative voices and perspectives that remain coherent if not always signposted for the reader. It is this elliptical structure that can be seen as echoing or paralleling a feature of Egoyan's cinema. It is the cinema of otherness and exile, or what Hamid

Naficy terms an 'accented film'. While the dominant cinema considers itself to be universal and finds it almost impossible to think of itself as having an accent, the 'accented film' is all too aware of its accent. It is the self-consciousness of not belonging. In Egoyan's film version, Felicia symbolises this otherness and dislocation in everything from her clothing to her faltering syntax, with its traces and echoes of her grandmother's language: 'I'm not sure am I in the right place.'

In Trevor's novel, the narrative often involves memories (both Hilditch's and Felicia's), as well as Hilditch's fantasies, which collide and meld, and Felicia's hopes and imaginings, which dissolve into each other. The novel's handling of time and space also involves shifts in time and perspective. In adapting the novel for the screen, Egoyan deploys one of his signature strategies – that of video technology – as a central narrative device. The visual style and structure of Egoyan's adaptation makes effective use of different visual registers, through which the different stories of Felicia and Hilditch are mediated. This presents and provides a level of reflexivity which involves the audience in some of the issues which emerge in his films as he dislodges mainstream cinema's conventions.

Egoyan has proposed that the camera functions as a modern chorus, seeing it as: 'a redefinition of the Greek chorus. Maybe the lens is the new chorus for our drama, it is the thing which comments on the actions of the principal actors.'[80] His use of video/home movie footage is embedded in the narrative syntax – as a reflexive and reflective tool – pulling viewers into and through the narrative while also breaking up the smooth flow of more conventional cinema. Media technologies which have become increasingly domesticated – providing records of family events and experiences – open up a certain kind of tension for him: 'If you record, you miss out on participating directly in the event, because it is filtered through a lens.[81] It is this activity of recording, of building a series of electronic memories, which gives an ambiguous charge to the visual style of

Felicia's Journey, especially in the contrasting styles through which we are given access to Hilditch's memories and Felicia's past.

The role of the image – specifically the photograph – in memory has a substantial history. Writing in 1859, Oliver Wendell Holmes described photography as 'the mirror with a memory'.[82] More recently, Roland Barthes in *Camera Lucida*[83] explores the relationship between photography and memory not only as image but in his experience of the photograph as an object. Barthes describes his search for a photograph of his mother: 'There I was, alone in the apartment where she had died, looking at these pictures of my mother, one by one, under the lamp, gradually moving back in time with her, looking for the truth of the face I had loved. And I found it.' And he continues:

> A sort of umbilical cord links the body of the photographed thing to my gaze: light, though impalpable, is here a carnal medium, a skin I share with anyone who has been photographed . . . the loved body is immortalised by the mediation of a precious metal . . . (Hence the winter garden photograph, however pale, is for me the treasury of rays which emanated from my mother as a child, from her hair, her skin, her dress, her gaze, on that day.[84]

For Barthes, the power of the photograph is not only in looking at his mother's face but the physical experience he can feel as he touches the fading images. Hilditch's search for his mother also takes the form of a mediated image, but in his case it is not exclusively the still photograph – instead he favours the electronically produced moving image on video tape. As noted, Hilditch's house has a museum-like aspect and many of the objects have a retro quality, including the television, record-player and telephone. The large kitchen in which he prepares his meals also exudes a strong period feel. Yet here in the kitchen, he has installed a video recorder and monitor, which he uses to replay videos of his mother's TV career. Watching his mother nightly in grainy black-and-white images, Hilditch interacts with the images – assuming control of the image (and attempting control of his mother's memory), focusing his (and her) gaze via the opera glasses (those opera glasses taking on the values of a relic, redolent of memories of a night at the opera with his mother) and obsessively imitating her gestures. We are also privy to some out-takes in the production, those errors drawing our attention to the necessary artifice associated with the creation of the very images we are presented with. And since this is Hilditch's most direct access to memories of his mother, it also poses questions about the fragility of his memory – personal, private, subjective – especially when considering Hilditch's mangled psyche. While for Barthes there is a physical pleasure in recalling his mother's physical presence, the video recall for Hilditch, paradoxically, is a necessary barrier, evoking the desire/repulsion of their relationship. We are given access to his intense viewing of her programmes, which both engage and punish him – the replay of his mother's irritation, his gagging on the liver – articulating his endless desire for her in the present and in the past.

As a narrative device, these video replays, with their characteristic graininess, bring a reflexive quality to the film, which is further layered in the use of other visual material – the portentous shot of Felicia captured in Hilditch's side-view mirror and the curious images of her legs and feet – the meaning of which is only gradually revealed in its full sinister significance. Using opera glasses, Hilditch indulges his voyeuristic impulse, but now his focus is on Felicia as we realise he has used a hidden camera to record his meeting with her earlier in the day. The soundtrack dialogue explains and anchors the meaning of the video image; and, later, labelled 'Irish Eyes', his surveillance footage of Felicia is added to the collection which forms his video archive. The installation of a hidden camera in the hump-backed green car, which he uses to capture and frame the girls, is a further curiosity in his character. In the novel, he calls them up through his internal Memory Lane. In the film, this translates into a video archive of his victims, a record of his voyeurism and his surveillance. Appealing in his friendly overtures, the casting of Hoskins as Hilditch adds a further disarming dimension and causes a shock when we become aware of the hidden surveillance camera and the archive of his victims, stored in a room in his house. The series of 'talking heads' of the girls in his archive were also re-imagined and entitled 'Evidence' and included in 'Notorious – Alfred Hitchcock and Contemporary Art' at MOMA, Oxford, in 1999, giving further intertextual shadings to the film.

Egoyan's tendency for reflexivity in the screen image and in narrative flow has invariably attracted the term 'postmodern' to describe his cinema. Jonathan Romney usefully elaborates this categorisation of

> Egoyan's status as an eminently postmodern filmmaker, if we understand the postmodern experience – as described by critic Fredric Jameson – to be a matter less of alienation than of fragmentation. Egoyan's films put us in the position of Jameson's postmodern viewer, 'called upon to do the impossible, namely, to see all the screens at once, in their radical and random difference . . .' To put it another way, Egoyan wants us to be absorbed in his dramas and to remain critically detached from them.[85]

In *Felicia's Journey*, the narrative is structured through the different visual registers, inviting us to view and review the tale (its teller and mode of telling), prompting us to question the perspectives rather than undermining them totally. In this way, Hilditch's outward affability conceals his creepiness, which is only gradually revealed, although visual cues (such as that mentioned above) have been made available to viewers. The unreliability of the video memories (which have been staged and directed in a TV studio) also draws attention to the nature and unreliability of memory, which is nebulous, shifting and personal. Staying with the notion of the postmodern, cinema and the nature of memory, Linda Hutcheon provides an illuminating assessment in the context of the visual and narrative style of *Felicia's Journey:* 'It [postmodernism] does not deny the existence of the past, it does question whether we can ever know that past other than through its textualised remains.'[86]

It is the 'textualised remains' of Hilditch's past which we share with him, from the video archive of Gala and the cabinet of curiosities of his home to the popular songs which he plays obsessively, filling the house with other people's voices (as he has filled the house with other people's garments and possessions). Hilditch is shown to rely heavily on material objects to fabricate his life and as a means to gain access to his past. Although his mother is dead, he brings her to life through the video replay (keeping her alive *à la* Norman Bates). Through his fussy and fastidious duplicity (a make-believe wife whose clothes we see on the drying rail; the elaborate flower arrangements for a funeral that will never take place), viewers are invited to assess the other objects, texts and roles which he uses.

The high degree of reflexivity (different screens, framed portraits, visual styles) in Egoyan's film conforms to what Hutcheon categorises as postmodern with a 'doubled discourse', which 'calls attention to the ideological constructions – through representation – of subjectivity and of the way we know history both personal and public'.[87] Egoyan's visual layering is again foregrounded in the hospital, where we see the TV screen image of Rita Hayworth's Salome, reminding us of the power of the image, of cinema's legacy in forming our culture, drawing viewers into the layers of visual styles, inviting questions as to the the potential subtextual significance of such juxtapositions.

The contrast between Hilditch's relationship to his past in the present and that of Felicia illustrates this double discourse through the visual style. Punctuating the narrative flow are Felicia's recollections and dreams of her errant lover and father of her child as well as the stark memories of her father's house with its nationalist rhetoric. Eschewing the conventional signposting indicating a dream or memory, Felicia's images are easily available to her. History and her past (for good or ill) are alive for Felicia and integrated into her everyday life (despite her displacement and disorientation in the alien urban space). Her father's voice reverberates with his rhetorical clichés, sounding like empty slogans which have parallels echoing in the futile pieties of the evangelical Miss Calligary, but she manages and negotiates these as part of her growth.

For Hilditch, however, his struggle to possess his past and his memories is bound up with video technology – always at a remove – in the black and white of the past, or the more lurid colour of a home movie, rather than the natural colour which characterises Felicia's memories. Egoyan has alluded to the different traditions which form Hilditch and Felicia – referring to the oral culture of Felicia's experience – and offers an equivalence in the visual registers which make available their memories.[88]

Narrative, Memory and Identity

During the film of *Felicia's Journey*, a series of flashbacks of 'talking heads' appears on screen of the girls whom Hilditch has befriended over time and whose images and stories he has recorded and collected on videotape through his hidden surveillance camera. At one point, one of them asks him: 'Why do you need my story?' As Hilditch collects the encounters with the various girls, he is also eagerly collecting their stories in the absence of any robust story of his own. Frequently, screen moments (from the Memory Lane video archive; the visual memories of his mother's performances, with his subsidiary role; an extract from *Salome*) disrupt the flow of the film's narrative, functioning not only at a visual level but also presenting narrative tangents and fragments which, at times, generate a subtext – Rita Hayworth as the fatal castrating woman whose appetite for a severed head is amply fulfilled – and elsewhere revealing glimpses of other narratives which remain incomplete. All are refracted and reflected through Hilditch's perspective in his desire for a narrative of his own.

Psychologist Jerome Bruner writes:

> Narrative organises not just memory, but the whole of human experience – not just life stories of the past, but all of one's life as it unfolds . . . narrative is an instrument of mind that constructs our notion of reality – the experience of life takes on meaning when we interact with it as an ongoing story, as our story.[89]

Egoyan's reflexive dimension on several visual and narrative levels fractures Hilditch's narrative and offers a parallel to his fractured sense of identity. His attempts to fashion a narrative of his own are revealed to be frail and timid (he forgets his lie about Ada's death even as he is carrying the large funeral wreaths he ordered to enhance the deception); he is shown to have a ritualistic reliance on mediated images and memories of his childhood with his mother; he has an obsessive drive to collect the girls on film/video, each named (as a story) and labelled for storage. And although he is shown interacting with the replayed image of his mother on screen, the ritualistic repetition signifies his time-warped existence rather than an ongoing dynamic. Writing in *The Neurology of Narrative*,[90] Young and Saver refer to states of narrative impairment and assert that 'these conditions reveal that narrative framing and recall of experience is a dynamic, variable and vulnerable process'. They continue:

> Modern neuroscience has demonstrated that retrieving memories is not a simple act of accessing a storehouse of ready-made photos in a stable neural album, preserved with complete fidelity to the moment of their formation. Rather, each act of recall is a re-creation, drawing upon multiple, dynamically changing modular fragments to shape a new mosaic.[91]

Hilditch's recall, predicated as it is on mediated forms and seemingly trapped in repetition of location and space (physically and emotionally – he has lived in the house since his mother died), lacks the dynamic that might allow him to interact with his memories as an ongoing story. Whether labelled and packaged in his storehouse (off the kitchen, stored alongside the shelves laden with boxes containing Gala-endorsed food processors) or as part of the museum-like house, Hilditch's house is packed with stories not his own, just as in the novel we learn that he, like a curator and colonial collector of the imperial age, has collected objects and memorabilia (not his own) and furnished his house with other people's worlds and narratives. Surrounded by fabrication and artifice, he has failed to construct any meaningful narrative of self, leaving him unaware or, as Egoyan suggests, in denial of his own evil doings. The elliptical style of the film frustrates Hilditch's attempts to make his narrative cohere. In the novel, this need for coherence is expressed through his constant search for external validation of his fantasies through being seen (with Felicia and the other girls) in public spaces such as cafés.

The film is informed by narrative as a fundamental structuring device of experience and memory as well as the way in which narrative processes are culturally embedded. Egoyan cites Cocteau's *Beauty and the Beast* (1946) as an influence on *Felicia's Journey*, especially when it came to his depiction of Hilditch's house: 'My reference for that was Cocteau's *Beauty and the Beast*. She's expelled from this village by her father's actions and driven to this dark castle where she encounters this beast who falls in love with her.'[92] Along with the explicit reference to the story of Salome, he has also referred to the story of Bluebeard's Castle, indicative of how narrative forms and ways of telling structure our wider experience and involve the viewer/reader. It also points to the structuring influence of the folktale/fairytale in popular culture and the constant recycling and re-working of those themes in film. Egoyan's reference to the folktale has a certain pertinence in the wider context and resonances of

Felicia's story. The tendency to personify Ireland as female (often as a beautiful young woman bound to a brutish husband – perfidious Albion) lends itself to the morphology *of Beauty and the Beast*.

That Felicia is Beauty and some form of angel is also signalled on the soundtrack. For Hilditch, who has been a marginal narrative agent throughout his life – a bit player in his mother's performances, discarded by the young girls who want to move on and advance their own stories – Felicia is his angelic helper. Externally validated through his part in Felicia's story as told to Miss Calligary, he begins to tell his own story, falteringly, assuming his identity – even confessing to his theft of her money. Having begun to narrate his life, to speak his identity, 'I am a catering manager. I am a respectable man. Hilditch I am called' (the last phrase redolent of fairytale/pantomine style), he appears to realise his crimes and hangs himself as his narrative closure.[93]

In his director's commentary on the DVD version, Egoyan refers to the theme of fertility, which he chose to amplify through the opening images of various types of eggs. Although not as explicit as a theme in the novel, the notion of fertility offers a commentary on the source material, on the way in which fertility as growth/potential has been negated by several characters in the novel. If the 'bad mother' tends to dominate Hilditch's story and Lysaght's mother offers little respite from the negative view of the possessive mother whose 'love for [her] son [was] gentle as a cancer', the fathers of the novel and film are either entirely absent (in the case of Hilditch and Lysaght) or exhibit a brutal cruelty (Felicia's father calls her a 'hooer', forcing her to leave his house). A persistence of memory of the father's futility into the next generation comes through Johnny Lysaght's desertion of Felicia. Like father, like son. At the close of the film, Felicia reads a letter in voiceover to Mrs Lysaght, underlining the theme of fertility, which in this case has been arrested, 'Your grandchild was never born, Mrs Lysaght', providing a closure to the theme visualised in the opening scenes. For Hilditch, too, there is no continuance of his lineage – following his role in Felicia's abortion, perhaps. The house, with its collections of memorabilia, 'belongs to the state, there being no inheritor' (*FJ*, p. 203) – the final closure, the end of the line.

The representation of Hilditch's death in the novel acts as a summation of his wretched existence:

> No one passing by in Duke of Wellington Road, no hurrying housewife, or child, or business person, or one who can see Number Three from the top of the buses that ply to and fro on a nearby street, has reason to wonder about this house or its single occupant. (*FJ*, p. 200)

Trevor also indicates an eloquent sympathy for his character: 'No one passing is aware that a catering manager from a factory, well liked and without enemies, is capable of suffering no more' (*FJ*, p. 200). With cinematic fluency, the reader is led to Hilditch's final act, where he is now 'suspended from the single ham hook in the wooden ceiling by a length of electric flex' (*FJ*, p. 201).

As Felicia's journey ends in the novel, we are aware of her changed role and the transformation that has occurred. Her compassion is assured for that 'wretched, awful man, poor mockery of a human creature, with his pebble spectacles and the tiny hands that didn't match the rest of him, his executioner's compulsion' (*FJ*, p. 211). And although vengeance is perpetrated by her brothers on Johnny Lysaght, leaving him 'insensible in the dark by the memorial statue' (*FJ*, p. 202), Felicia is now far away from this kind of savage justice, having achieved a sense and knowledge of self.

As in the novel, the film's resolution of Felicia's narrative journey has also brought her to a certain realisation as the woman who knew too much, now finding herself in the role of the final girl.[94] Previously seeming to Hilditch like his 'special angel', she now assumes the role of redeeming angel. Finally free of Hilditch, liberated from the narrow rhetoric of her father's vision, released from the dogma of

Miss Calligary's paradise and the futile fantasy of a life with the errant Lysaght, Felicia emerges from her journey with little baggage, and also takes on the role of recording angel – naming the names of the lost girls as a memorial litany.

The final scenes show her in a garden (and not the extravagant picture-book confections favoured by Miss Calligary). Away from the visual claustrophobia of her homeland, beyond the towering buildings and architectures of industrial Britain, the camera finds her in a public garden in the centre of a city of tall buildings in a significantly different space to those she has come from and passed through. Planting bulbs, she is shown content and engaged. She is also an agent of renewal and growth. In a departure from the novel – in which Felicia becomes a bag lady, aimlessly moving from place to place – the film's ending arguably ties in with Trevor's recurrent notion of compassion and renewal; the slow movement of the camera in the final scenes of the film locate Felicia in the agora, where trees, plants and buildings co-exist, serene in her own small Eden.[95]

However, such is the openness of the film version that it gives the possibility of a wide range of different readings. For example, writing of Egoyan's endings, Geoff Pevere asserts that his films display a marked tendency towards an impossible optimism, which he reads as a search for home and stability: 'Egoyan's films have consistently been marked by a kind of melodramatic pose of closure, moments of final punctuation so archly articulated that they seem to mock the very idea of happy endings and thus of home itself.'[96] In this context he reads Egoyan's closure of *Felicia's Journey* as highly ironic, as a form of desperate excess in which Felicia fantasises in her nomadic wanderings amid the derelicts and the other homeless of the city. Perhaps the final irony is that the text itself is so nomadic: it refuses closure, as it makes its own journey from medium to medium, reader to reader, and culture to culture.

CREDITS

....

Title:	*Felicia's Journey*
Director	Atom Egoyan
Release Year:	1999

Cast:

Bob Hoskins	Hilditch
Arsinée Khanjian	Gala
Elaine Cassidy	Felicia
Sheila Reid	Iris
Nizwar Karanj	Sidney
Ali Yassine	Customs Officer
Peter McDonald	Johnny
Kriss Dosanjh	Salesman
Gerard McSorley	Felicia's Father
Marie Stafford	Felicia's Great-Grandmother (as Maire Stafford)
Gavin Kelty	Shay Mulroone
Brid Brennan	Mrs Lysaght
Mark Hadfield	Television Director
Danny Turner	Young Hilditch
Susan Parry	Salome
Claire Benedict	Miss Calligary
Jean Marlow	Old Woman
Sidney Cole	Ethiopian
Barry McGovern	Gatherer
Sandra Voe	Jumble Sale Woman
Leila Hoffman	Bag Lady
Bob Mason	Jimmy
Emma Powell	Clinic Receptionist
Julie Cox	Marcia Tibbits
Nicki Murphy	Lost Girl
Kelly Brailsford	Lost Girl
Polly York	Lost Girl
Gem Durham	Lost Girl
Kerry Stacey	Lost Girl
Laura Chambers	Lost Girl
Bianca McKenzie	Lost Girl
Ladene Hall	Lost Girl

Bruce Davey	Producer
Karen Glasser	Associate producer
Ralph Kamp	Executive producer
Robert Lantos	Co-producer
Paul Tucker	Executive producer
Mychael Danna	Original music
Jimmy Duncan	Non-Original music (song 'My Special Angel')
Mary Bond	(song 'More Than Ever')
Kate Bush	(song 'The Sensual World')
Vincent Dipaolo	(song 'More Than Ever')
Paul Sarossy	Director of photography
Susan Shipton	Film editing
Leo Davis	Casting
Jim Clay	Production design
Chris Seagers	Art direction
Sandy Powell	Costume design
Miri Ben-Schlomo	Hair assistant (as Miri Ben-Shlomo)
Miri Ben-Schlomo	Make-up assistant (as Miri Ben-Shlomo)
Stevie Hall	Hair designer
Morag Ross	Makeup designer
Ted Morley	Production supervisor
Matthew Baker	Second assistant director
Danny McGrath	Third assistant director (as Dan McGrath)
David J. Webb	First assistant director (as David Webb)
Malcolm Bensted	Storeman
John Bohan	Construction coordinator
Peter Dorme	Draughtsman
Gill Ducker	Production buyer
Paul Duff	Stand-by carpenter
Heidi Gibb	Art department assistant
Jo Graysmark	Location art director
Bill Hargreaves	Chargehand stand-by props
David Mears	Stand-by painter
Brian Mitchell	Stand-by stagehand
Steve Payne	Dressing props
Graeme Purdy	Property master
Pippa Rawlinson	Art department stand-by

Bob Sherwood	Stand-by props
Jan Spoczynski	Draughtsman
Robin Heinson	Chargehand painter (uncredited)
Colin Baxter	Associate sound effects editor
Eric A. Christoffersen	Stereo sound consultant: Dolby
Ed Colyer	ADR mixer
Sue Conly	Dialogue editor (as Sue Conley)
Keith Elliott	Foley recordist
Keith Elliott	Sound re-recording mixer
James Harris	Sound assistant
Peter Kelly	Sound re-recording mixer
Andy Malcolm	Foley artist
Timothy Mehlenbacher	Assistant sound editor
Steve Munro	Sound designer (as Steven Munro)
Daniel Pellerin	Sound re-recording mixer
John Pitt	Sound maintenance engineer
Steve Pollet	Assistant sound editor
Tim Roberts	ADR editor
Brian Simmons	Production sound mixer
Stephen Stepanic	Assistant music engineer
David Drainie Taylor	Dialogue editor
John F. Thompson	Foley assistant
Rebecca Wright	Foley assistant
Sharon Zupancic	Foley assistant
Colin Skeaping	Stunt coordinator
Alison Bage	Unit nurse
Sophie Baker	Still photographer
Naoise Barry	Co-location manager: Ireland
Daniel Blackman	Musician: viola
Debbie Brodie	Home economist
Ian Buckley	Grip
Neil Chaplin	Production accountant
Frederick Chiverton	Music consultant
Marilyn Clarke	Production coordinator
Andrew Cooke	Co-location manager: Birmingham
Alison Crosbie	Casting assistant
Kate Crossan	Singer
Ira Curtis-Coleman	Specialist video (as Ira Curtis Coleman)
Chris Dale	Camera trainee
Nick Daubeny	Location manager

Tim de Malmanche	Unit driver
Peter Devlin	Unit driver
Penny Dyer	Dialogue coach
Shaun Evans	Clapper loader
Warren Ewen	Electrician
Chuck Finch	Gaffer (as Robert 'Chuck' Finch)
Steven Finch	Electrician (as Steve Finch)
Sammy Fonfe	Utility stand-in
Willie Fonfe	Transportation coordinator
Michele Francis	Second assistant editor
Anya Gripari	Floor runner
Graham Hall	Focus puller
Pippa Hall	Casting: youth
Chris Hinton	Color timer
Keith Horsley	Unit driver
Bridget Hunt	Musician: violin
Nigel Kirton	Steadicam operator
Ron Korb	Musician: flute
Brad Larner	Steadicam assistant
Cheryl Leigh	Script supervisor
Andrew Lockington	Assistant to composer
Simon Lucas	Electrician
Billy Merrell	Best boy
Alison Odell	Assistant to director
Alison Odell	Assistant to producer
Sammy Pasha	Assistant: Bob Hoskins (as Sammy Pascha)
Michaela Piper	Publicist
Louisa Rawlins	Production office assistant
Lyndy Rist	Assistant accountant
Valerie Rosewell	Assistant accountant
Lorraine Samuel	Second assistant editor
Mark Sanger	Second assistant editor
Clare Scholtz	Musician: oboe
Debbie Scott	Assistant to costume designer
Ron Searles	Music engineer
Ameene Shishakly	Musician: clarinet
Sunita Singh	Wardrobe assistant
Mark Somner	Co-location manager: London
Clare Spragge	Wardrobe supervisor
Mark Stokes	Second assistant editor

Angelique Toews	Musician: violin
Sophie Tucker	Floor assistant
Simone Urdl	Assistant: Mr Egoyan
Sarah Walden	Contact: London
Bonnie F. Watkins	Assistant: Mr Davey
Johanna Weinstein	Title designer
David Weller	Stand-by rigger (as Dave Weller)
Janet Willis	Tutor
George Worley	Generator operator
Kirk Worthington	Musician: cello
Tai Zimmer	Assistant editor
Ian Clarke	Vehicle technician (uncredited)
Andrew Rosen	Production assistant: Alliance Atlantis (uncredited)
Clare Spragge	Costume supervisor (uncredited)
Simon St Laurent	Opticals: Film Opticals (uncredited)
Sean Thornton	Picture vehicle technician (uncredited)

Notes

1. William Trevor, *Mrs Eckdorf in O'Neill's Hotel* (London: Bodley Head, 1969).

2. The origins of the term 'Celtic Tiger' are unclear. It may have been coined by the US investment bankers Morgan Stanley in 1994, though it took a number of years to pass into common currency. See Peader Kirby, *The Celtic Tiger in Distress: Growth With Inequality in Ireland* (Basingstoke: Palgrave, 2002), and *Reinventing Ireland: Culture, Society and the Global Economy*, eds. Peadar Kirby, Luke Gibbons and Michael Cronin (London: Pluto, 2002).

3. The Central Statistics Office notes in its website's comments (<http://www.cso.ie>) on the country's 2002 Census: 'The high emigration during the 1950s was responsible for the historically low population level of 2.8 million recorded in 1961. Population levels began to rise again during the 1960s mainly as a result of the decline in net outward migration. The reversal in net migration from outward to inward during the 1970s alongside an increase in births led to an overall population increase of just over 465,000 between 1971 and 1981. Net outward migration resumed again during the early 1980s and, coupled with a decline in births, resulted in a moderation in the rate of overall population increase. The sharp increase in net outward migration in the second half of the 1980s, along with a continued fall in the number of births, resulted in a small population loss between 1986 and 1991. In the 1991–1996 period there was a further decline in the average annual natural increase due to the declining birth rate. However, there was a change around once again in the pattern of migration, with a small net inflow recorded. The most recent intercensal period has seen the average annual natural increase revert to the level attained during the late 1980s. Coupled with historically high net inward migration this has led to an annual average population increase on a par with that achieved during the 1970s.'

4. Central Statistics Office, Dublin.

5. Alan Parker, quoted in Andrew Higson, *English Heritage, English Cinema: Costume Drama Since 1980* (Oxford: Oxford University Press, 2003), p. 68. For extensive discussion of adaptation and the 'heritage film', see also *Film/Literature/Heritage A Sight and Sound Reader*, ed. Ginette Vincendeau (London: BFI, 2001).

6. Lance Corporal Ian Malone, aged 28, a Dubliner, was killed by sniper fire on Sunday 6 April 2003 in the battle of Basra in Iraq. Malone was

interviewed on RTÉ television while on leave in November 2002. Speaking about his career he said: 'At the end of the day, I'm just abroad doing a job. People go on saying Irish men died for our freedom. They did. They died to give men like me the freedom to choose what I want to do. I have sworn an oath of allegiance and I can't walk away from it. I will stick by it. Dishonouring that contract would be far more disloyal than joining the British army.'

7. Scott Tobias, 'The Director of *The Sweet Hereafter*, *Exotica* and the New *Felicia's Journey* Talks to *The Onion*', *theonionavclub.com*, 17 November 1999, Vol. 35, No. 42.

8. Dolores MacKenna, *William Trevor: the Writer and His Work* (Dublin: New Island Books, 1999), p. 1.

9. Monika Maurer, 'A Quick Chat with Atom Egoyan', *Kamera.co.uk*, November 1998.

10. Maurer, 'A Quick Chat', 1998.

11. Atom Egoyan, director's commentary, *Felicia's Journey*, DVD, 1999.

12. Tobias, *The Onion* interview, 1999.

13. William Trevor, *Felicia's Journey* (London: Viking, 1994), p. 16. Page numbers from this edition will be used throughout.

14. Felim MacDermott and Declan McGrath, *Screencraft/Screenwriting* (Sussex: Rotovision, 2003).

15. For example, see George Sanderson and Frank MacDonald, *Marshall McLuhan: the Man and His Message* (Colorado: Fulcrum, 1989).

16. *Here's Looking at You Kid: Ireland Goes to the Pictures*, eds. Stephanie McBride and Roddie Flynn (Dublin: 1996), p. 128.

17. *Subtitles*, eds. Atom Egoyan and Ian Balfour (Alphabet City Media/MIT Press, 2004), p. 21.

18. Hamid Naficy, 'Epistolarity and Textuality in Accented Films', in Egoyan and Balfour, p. 134.

19. <http://www.pub.umich.edu/daily/1999>.

20. Jonathan Romney, 'Return of the Mighty Atom', *Guardian* (24 September 1999).

21. User comments by Birmingham resident 'bob the moo' on the Internet Movie Database film website IMDB.com, 30 September 2003: 'I must admit that much of my interest in this film was held by the fact that it was filmed partly in my adopted home town of Birmingham. Set around Nechells we have the gloomy presence of the gas works, the tower blocks of Aston and the industrial estate landscape of both. Locals will also recognise the bottom of Gravely Hill as the location of the B&B and the external of The Barton Arms pub and The Electric Cinema (a supporter of Egoyan's films!).'

22. David Lodge, 'Adapting Nice Work for Television', *Novel Images: Literature in Performance*, ed. Peter Reynolds (London: Routledge, 1993).

23. Brian McFarlane, *Novel to Film: an Introduction to the Theory of Adaptation* (Oxford: Clarendon Press, 1996), p. 8.

24. For an incisive and illuminating account of this concept, see Graham Allen, *Intertextuality* (London: Routledge, 2000).

25. Italo Calvino, *If on a Winter's Night a Traveller* (1979; London: Minerva, 1981), p. 7.

26. Alan Powers, *Front Cover: Great Book Jacket and Cover Design* (London: Mitchell Beazley, 2001).

27. John Ellis, *Visible Fictions: Cinema/Television/Video* (London: Routledge and Kegan Paul, 1982).

28. For a humorous reflection on postmodernist culture and book covers, see Gilbert Adair, *The Postmodernist Always Rings Twice: Reflections on Culture in the 90s* (London: Fourth Estate, 1992), p. 19.

29. Tony McAuley (dir.), *William Trevor: Hidden Ground* (UK: BBC Northern Ireland, 1990).

30. For Trevor's extensive survey of the theme of landscape, history and literature, see William Trevor, *A Writer's Ireland: Landscape in Literature* (London: Thames and Hudson, 1984).

31. Martin Gale: Paintings (RHA Catalogue, 2004), p. 25.

32. For a comprehensive list of screen adaptations of Trevor's fiction, see MacKenna, pp. 240–241.

33. MacKenna, p. 157.

34. For an exploration of this theme, see Fintan O'Toole, *The Lie of the Land*, catalogue essay (Dublin: Gallery of Photography, 1995).

35. Novels such as Mrs Henry Wood's *East Lynne* (1861), Mary Elizabeth Braddon's *Lady Audley's Secret* (1862), Wilkie Collins's *The Woman in White* (1859) and *The Moonstone* (1868), Charles Dickens's *Bleak House* (1852) and R. L. Stevenson's *Dr Jekyll and Mr Hyde* (1886).

36. MacKenna, p. 169.

37. For an extensive discussion of the origins and role of the imperial archive and its portrayal in literature in the works of Rudyard Kipling, Erskine Childers, H. G. Wells and Bram Stoker, see Thomas Richards, *The Imperial Archive* (London: Verso, 1993).

38. Richards, p. 4.

39. Richards, p. 15.

40. For a discussion of this theme within a post-colonial frame, see Liam Harte and Lance Pettitt, 'States of Dislocation: William Trevor's

Felicia's Journey and Maurice Leitch's *Gilchrist'*, in *Comparing Post-Colonial Literatures: Dislocations*, eds. Ashok Bery and Patricia Murray (London: Macmillan Press, 2000). See also Richards, pp. 19–25.

41. Mary Fitzgerald-Hoyt, *William Trevor: Re-imagining Ireland* (Dublin: The Liffey Press, 2003).

42. There is an extensive body of writing on the topic of adaptation, e.g. Morris Beja, *Film and Literature* (Longman, 1979); George Bluestone, *Novels into Film* (UCA Press, 1957); Brian McFarlane, *Novel to Film* (Oxford, 1996); John Orr and Colin Nicholson, *Cinema and Fiction: New Modes of Adapting 1950–1990* (Edinburgh University Press, 1992); Robert Stam and Alessandra Raengo, *Literature and Film: a Guide to the Theory and Practice of Film Adaptation* (Blackwell Publishing, 2004); *Literature Through Film: Realism, Magic, and the Art of Adaptation* (Blackwell Publishing, 2004).

43. Lodge, pp. 191–203.

44. Egoyan, director's commentary.

45. For an account of this case, see Nell McCafferty, *A Woman to Blame: the Kerry Babies Case* (Dublin: Attic Press, 1985); see also Joanne Hayes, *My Story* (Dingle: Brandon Books, 1985).

46. *FJ*, p. 99.

47. See Anne Crilly (dir.), *Mother Ireland* (Channel 4, 1988), a televison documentary which explores this myth.

48. For a discussion of poetic portrayal of Ireland as female, see Elizabeth Butler Cullingford, 'Thinking of Her as Ireland: Yeats, Pearse and Heaney', *Textual Practice*, Vol. 4, No. 1 (1990). See also Fitzgerald-Hoyt, chapter 6, 'De-Colleenising Ireland'.

49. See Tania Modleski, *The Women Who Knew Too Much* (New York and London: Methuen, 1988), chapter 7.

50. Anon., *Publisher's Weekly* (1994), cited in <http://search.barnesand noble.com/booksearch/isbninquiry.asp?isbn=9780140290219>.

51. See Fitzgerald-Hoyt, chapter 7. See also McBride and Flynn, p. 128.

52. Michael Dibdin, *The Picador Book of Crime Writing* (London: Picador, 1994).

53. Dibdin, p. 3.

54. T. S. Eliot, quoted in Dibdin, pp. 207–208.

55. For other accounts of the genre, see Julian Symons, *Bloody Murder: From the Detective Story to the Crime Novel* (1985); Ian Ousby, *The Crime and Mystery Book* (1997); Martin Priestman, *Crime Fiction: From Poe to the Present* (1998).

56. *Barnes and Noble* website <http://search.barnesandnoble.com/booksearch/isbninquiry.asp?isbn=9780140290219>.

57. See also Stephanie McBride, 'Intermedia: Knocking Down the Museum Walls, *Irish Times* (23 August 2001), p. 12.

58. For an extensive account of literary and artistic influences and relations, see 'Hitchcock and Art: Fatal Coincidences' (Pompidou Centre, 2001).

59. See Jane Caputi, *The Age of Sex Crime* (Ohio: Bowling Green State University Popular Press, 1987); Jane Caputi, 'The Sexual Politics of Murder', *Gender and Society*, Vol. 3, No. 4 (1989); Jane Caputi, 'The New Founding Fathers: the Lore and Lure of the Serial Killer in Contemporary Culture', *Journal of American Culture*, Vol. 13, No. 3, (1990); Mark Seltzer, 'The Serial Killer as a Type of Person', in *The Horror Reader*, ed. Ken Gelder (London: Routledge, 2000), which is an extract from Mark Seltzer, *Serial Killers* (London: Routledge, 1998).

60. Thomas Harris, *The Silence of the Lambs* (New York: St Martin's Press, 1988), p. 258.

61. Cynthia Fuchs, interview with Atom Egoyan, *Pop Matters* <http://www.popmatters.com/film/interviews/egoyan-atom.html>.

62. See, for example, Alan Beardsworth and Teresa Keil, *Sociology on the Menu: an Invitation to the Study of Food and Society* (London: Routledge, 1997), pp. 47–70; Claude Levi-Strauss, 'The Culinary Triangle'; Mary Douglas, 'Deciphering a Meal', in *Food and Culture: a Reader*, eds. Carole Counihan and Penny Van Esterik (London: Routledge, 1997).

63. Mary Douglas, *Purity and Danger: an Analysis of Concepts of Pollution and Taboo* (London: Allen and Unwin, 1966).

64. For example, the significance of eating and cooking in the subgenre of food films such as *Tampopo, Like Water for Chocolate, Strawberry and Chocolate, Eat Drink Man Woman, The Wedding Banquet, Chocolat.*

65. David Bell and Gill Valentine, Consuming Geographies: We Are Where We Eat (London: Routledge, 1997).

66. Margaret Visser, quoted in Bell and Valentine, p. 52.

67. Deborah Lupton, quoted in Bell and Valentine, p. 52.

68. Jonathan Demme (dir.), *The Silence of the Lambs* (1990).

69. Modleski, p. 107.

70. Modleski, p. 107.

71. Julia Kristeva, *Powers of Horror*, cited in Modleski, pp. 3, 13.

72. See a discussion of Hitchcock's ambivalence in Modleski, p. 107.

73. Dennis Potter, talking to the *Evening Standard* about his TV drama *Pennies From Heaven*, quoted in Humphrey Carpenter, *Dennis Potter: the Authorized Biography* (London: Faber and Faber, 1998), p. 348.

74. Atom Egoyan, quoted in Maurer, 'A Quick Chat', 1998.

75. In common with many Irish songs, there are several versions in different regions/singers. 'Tiocfaidh an Samhradh' describes the seasonal renewal which links with the wish for the return of a true love.

76. MacKenna.

77. Naficy, p. 136.

78. Mark Kermode, 'Controlling Interests', *The Independent*, cited in Jonathan Romney, *Atom Egoyan* (London: BFI, 2003).

79. Tobias (1999).

80. Egoyan, quoted in Romney, *Atom Egoyan*, p. 3.

81. Egoyan, quoted in Romney, *Atom Egoyan*, p. 5.

82. Oliver Wendell Holmes, 'The Stereoscope and the Stereograph', *The Atlantic Monthly* (June 1859), reprinted in *Photography: Essays and Images*, ed. Beaumont Newhall (MOMA: New York, 1980).

83. Roland Barthes, *Camera Lucida* (London: Flamingo, 1984).

84. Barthes, *Camera Lucida*, pp. 81–82.

85. Romney, *Atom Egoyan*, p. 2.

86. Linda Hutcheon, *A Poetics of Postmodernism: History, Theory, Fiction* (London: Routledge, 1988).

87. Hutcheon.

88. Atom Egoyan, director's commentary, *Felicia's Journey*, DVD.

89. Jerome Bruner, 'The Narrative Construction of Reality', *Critical Inquiry*, Vol. 18 (1991), 1–21.

90. Kay Young and Jeffrey Saver, 'The Neurology of Narrative', *SubStance*, Vol. 30, No. 1 (2001), 72–84. Young and Saver provide an account of the effects of various forms of brain injury on the ability to create and understand narrative. Crucially they argue that 'individuals who have lost the ability to construct narrative, however, have lost their selves'. For abstract, see <http://www.anth.ucsb.edu/projects/esm/YoungSaver.html>.

91. Young and Saver.

92. Maurer, 'A Quick Chat with Atom Egoyan', 1998.

93. Liam Harte and Lance Pettitt, 'States of Dislocation: William Trevor's *Felicia's Journey* and Maurice Leitch's *Gilchrist*' in *Comparing Post-Colonial Literatures: Dislocations*, eds. Ashok Bery and Patricia Murray (London: Macmillan, 2000). In their detailed essay, Harte and Pettitt present a compelling post-colonial reading of the novel, where Felicia represents an anti-colonial resistance who disrupts and finally destroys Hilditch's colonial identity. They suggest that 'Hilditch's final act of suicide may therefore be read as the implosion of an attenuated colonialism under the impact of a migrant

dissidence'. They also see Felicia's journey as a positive transformation 'to a new, migrant mode of being in the world'.

94. For an analysis of the concept of 'the final girl', see Carol J. Clover, *Men, Women and Chainsaws* (New York: Princeton University Press, 1993), in which she argues that the psycho-killer horror genre opens up subversive potential for gender politics. She asserts that viewers identify not only with the plight of the (mainly) female victims but also with the actions of the 'final girl', who survives and who is often the agent of the killer's demise.

95. Trevor's use of garden symbolism is discussed in MacKenna.

96. Geoff Pevere, 'Homeless: Atom Egoyan in Canada', in *Fifty Contemporary Filmmakers*, ed. Yvonne Tasker (London: Routledge, 2002), pp. 146–154.

Bibliography

Adair, Gilbert. *The Postmodernist Always Rings Twice: Reflections on Culture in the 90s.* London: Fourth Estate, 1992.

Allen, Graham. *Intertextuality.* London: Routledge, 2000.

Barthes, Roland. *Mythologies*, trans. A Lavers. London: Paladin, 1972.

——. *Camera Lucida: Reflections on Photography*, trans. R Howard. London: Jonathan Cape, 1981.

Barton, Ruth. *Irish National Cinema.* London and New York: Routledge, 2004.

Beardsworth, Alan, and Teresa Keil. *Sociology on the Menu: an Invitation to the Study of Food and Society.* London: Routledge, 1997.

Bell, David, and Gill Valentine. *Consuming Geographies: We Are Where We Eat.* London: Routledge, 1997.

Bery, Ashok, and Patricia Murray. Eds. *Dislocations: Comparing Post-Colonial Literatures.* London: Macmillan, 2000.

Bruner, J. 'The Narrative Construction of Reality'. *Critical Inquiry* (1991).

Butler Cullingford, Elizabeth. 'Thinking of Her as Ireland: Yeats, Pearse and Heaney'. *Textual Practice*, Vol. 4, No. 1 (1990).

Calvino, Italo. *If on a Winter's Night a Traveller.* London: Minerva, 1992.

Caputi, Jane. *The Age of Sex Crime.* Ohio: Bowling Green State University Popular Press, 1987.

——. 'The Sexual Politics of Murder'. *Gender and Society*, Vol. 3, No. 4 (1989).

Carpenter, Humphrey. *Dennis Potter: the Authorized Biography.* London: Faber and Faber, 1998.

Cartmell, Deborah, et al. Eds. *Pulping Fictions: Consuming Culture Across the Literature/Media Divide.* London: Pluto Press, 1996.

Cartmell, Deborah, and Imelda Whelehan. *Adaptations: From Text to Screen, Screen to Text.* London: Routledge, 1999.

Clover, Carol J. *Men, Women and Chainsaws.* New York: Princeton University Press, 1993.

Counihan, Carole, and Penny Van Esterik. Eds. *Food and Culture: a Reader.* London: Routledge, 1997.

Crilly, Anne. *Mother Ireland.* Documentary. Channel 4, 1988.

Dibdin, Michael. *The Picador Book of Crime Writing.* London: Picador, 1994.

Douglas, Mary. 'Deciphering a Meal', in *Food and Culture: a Reader,* ed. Carole Counihan and Penny Van Esterik. London: Routledge, 1997.

Ellis, John. *Visible Fictions, Cinema/Television/Video.* London: Routledge and Kegan Paul, 1982.

Fitzgerald-Hoyt, Mary. *William Trevor: Re-imagining Ireland*. Dublin: Liffey Press, 2003.

Gale, Martin. *Paintings, RHA Catalogue*. Dublin: 2004.

Gelder, Ken. Ed. *The Horror Reader*. London: Routledge, 2000.

Gibbons, Luke. *Transformations in Irish Culture*. Cork: Cork University Press, 1996.

Giddings, Robert, and Erica Sheen. *The Classic Novel: From Page to Screen*. Manchester: Manchester University Press, 2000.

Gould Boyum, Joy. *Double Exposure: Fiction into Film*. New York: New American Library, 1985.

Harris, Thomas. *The Silence of the Lambs*. New York: St Martin's Press, 1988.

Harte, Liam, and Lance Pettitt. 'States of Dislocation: William Trevor's *Felicia's Journey* and Maurice Leitch's *Gilchrist*', in *Dislocations: Comparing Post-Colonial Literatures*, ed. Ashok Bery and Patricia Murray. London: Macmillan, 2000.

Higson, Andrew. *English Heritage, English Cinema*. Oxford: Oxford University Press, 2003.

Hitchcock and Art: Fatal Coincidences. Paris: Pompidou Centre, 2001.

Hutcheon, Linda. *A Poetics of Postmodernism: History, Theory, Fiction*. London: Routledge, 1988.

Kirby, Peadar, Luke Gibbons and Michael Cronin. Eds. *Reinventing Ireland: Culture, Society and the Global Economy*. 2002.

Levi-Strauss, Claude, 'The Culinary Triangle', in *Food and Culture: a Reader*. Eds. Carole Counihan and Penny Van Esterik. London: Routledge, 1997.

McAuley, Tony (dir). *William Trevor: Hidden Ground*. Documentary. BBC Northern Ireland, 1990.

McBride, Stephanie, and Roddy Flynn. Eds. *Here's Looking at You Kid: Ireland Goes to the Pictures*. Dublin: Wolfhound Press, 1996.

McCafferty, Nell. *A Woman to Blame: the Kerry Babies Case*. Dublin: Attic Press, 1985.

MacDermott, Felim, and Declan McGrath. *Screencraft/Screenwriting*. Sussex: Rotovision, 2003.

McFarlane, Brian. *Novel to Film*. Oxford: Clarendon Press, 1996.

MacKenna, Dolores. *William Trevor: the Writer and His Work*. Dublin: New Island Books, 1999.

McLoone, Martin. *Irish Film: the Emergence of a Contemporary Cinema*. London: BFI, 2000.

Modleski, Tania. *The Women Who Knew Too Much: Hitchcock and Feminist Theory*. New York and London: Methuen, 1988.

Negra, Diane. 'Coveting the Feminine: Victor Frankenstein, Norman Bates and Buffalo Bill'. *Film and Literature Quarterly*, Vol. 24, No. 2 (1996).

Newhall, Beaumont. Ed. *Photography: Essays and Images, Illustrated Readings in the History of Photography*. London: Secker & Warburg, 1980.

Orr, John, and Colin Nicholson. *Cinema and Fiction: New Modes of Adapting 1950–1990*. Edinburgh: Edinburgh University Press, 1992.

O'Toole, Fintan. *The Lie of the Land*. Catalogue essay. Dublin: Gallery of Photography, 1995.

———. *After the Ball*. Dublin: New Island, 2003.

Ousby, Ian. *The Crime and Mystery Book: a Reader's Companion*. London: Thames and Hudson, 1997.

Pettitt, Lance. *Screening Ireland*. Manchester: Manchester University Press, 2000.

Pevere, Geoff. 'Homeless: Atom Egoyan in Canada', in *Fifty Contemporary Film-makers*, ed. Yvonne Tasker. London: Routledge, 2002.

Priestman, Michael. *Crime Fiction: From Poe to the Present*. London: Northcote House, in association with the British Council, 1998.

Reynolds, Peter. Ed. *Novel Images: Literature in Performance*. London: Routledge, 1993.

Richards, Thomas. *The Imperial Archive*. London: Verso, 1993.

Rockett, Kevin, Luke Gibbons and John Hill. *Cinema and Ireland*. London and Sydney: Croom Helm, 1989.

Romney, Jonathan. *Atom Egoyan*. London: BFI, 2003.

Sanderson, G., and F. MacDonald. Eds. *Marshall McLuhan: the Man and his Message*. Colorado: Fulcrum, 1989.

Seltzer, Mark. *Serial Killers*. London: Routledge, 1998.

Smith, Joan. *Hungry for You: From Cannibalism to Seduction – a Book of Food*. London: Vintage, 1997.

Symons, Julian. *Bloody Murder: From the Detective Story to the Crime Novel*. London: Macmillan, 1985.

———. *Criminal Practices: Symons on Crime Writing 60s to 90s*. London: Macmillan, 1994.

Trevor, William. *A Bit on the Side*. London: Penguin/Viking, 2004.

———. *After Rain*. London: Viking, 1996.

———. *The Collected Stories*. London: Viking, 1992.

———. *Felicia's Journey*. London: Viking, 1994.

———. *The News from Ireland and Other Stories*. London: Bodley Head, 1986.

——. *Outside Ireland: Selected Stories*. London: Penguin, 1992.

——. *A Writer's Ireland: Landscape in Literature*. London: Thames and Hudson, 1984.

Tschofen, Monique. 'Repetition, Compulsion and Representation in Atom Egoyan's Films', in *North of Everything: English Canadian Cinema since 1980*. Eds. William Beard and Jerry White. Alberta: University of Alberta Press, 2002. 166–183.

Vincendeau, Ginette. Ed. *Film/Literature/Heritage: A Sight and Sound Reader*. London: BFI, 2001.

Young, Kay, and Jeffrey Saver. 'The Neurology of Narrative'. *SubStance*. 94/5, Vol. 30, No. 1 (2001): 72–84.